with death
laughing

with death laughing

peter plate

a novel

SEVEN STORIES PRESS
New York • Oakland • London

Seven Stories Press
140 Watts Street
New York, NY 10013
sevenstories.com

Library of Congress Cataloging-in-Publication Data

Names: Plate, Peter, author.
Title: With death laughing : a novel / Peter Plate.
Description: First edition. | New York : Seven Stories Press, [2019]
Identifiers: LCCN 2018044587| ISBN 9781609809256 (paperback) |
  ISBN 9781609809263 (ebook)
Subjects: | BISAC: FICTION / Crime. | GSAFD: Noir fiction.
Classification: LCC PS3566.L267 W58 2019 | DDC 813/.54--dc23
LC record available at https://lccn.loc.gov/2018044587

Printed in the United States of America

9 8 7 6 5 4 3 2 1

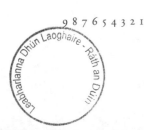

For
Jimmy and Donald,
Curt and Robert,
Glitter Doll, Dennis, Ricky,
and Montano Shoe Repair.

What the masses refuse to recognize is the fortuitousness that pervades reality.
—Hannah Arendt

PART ONE

THE BAD DAYS
WILL END

ONE

December is my favorite month. That's what I'm thinking when I look out my hotel room window and see a flurry of motion at the halfway house next door. A consumer—one of the house's residents—dances alone on the sidewalk with her arms held high, her costume jewelry bracelets a riot in the sunlight, an empty weightless plastic bag swirling on the pavement by her dirty, bare feet.

Sugar Child is the finest poetry I've seen in a long while.

I met Sugar Child earlier this morning while I was taking out the trash. Perching on the halfway house steps in a green spandex pantsuit, she's a revelation of reedy shoulders and bird-thin legs. A quality platinum wig frames her sharp grill. Her blood-rimmed brown eyes, ringed by artfully applied layers of blue mascara, examine me with x-ray intensity.

"Hey, daddy, you have a cigarette? No? Well, shit. You know I just got out of county jail. I did a year because I had no permits. I'm going to be here for ten days, then I got to find me a treatment program. But right now I want to party. Uh, you want a date? I don't do young guys. I do older men like you. Easier to handle. You interested?"

I'm in my underwear, too shy to flirt. "No, baby, I have to go to work in a little bit. Maybe some other time."

"Okay, daddy. I'll be waiting for you."

Quicker than a hummingbird, she lunges at me, planting a hard, cough-syrupy kiss on my mouth. An anvil of a kiss. Then she whirls away into the house.

I'm still looking out the window, reliving this memory, getting lost in its creaminess, when it's interrupted by a social worker rocketing out of the halfway house. He scuttles partway down the steps, stabbing the air with his clipboard. "Sugar Child! You need to stop dancing! What the hell is wrong with you! Get inside and take your meds! You're hours behind schedule!"

Ignoring him, Sugar Child does a fandango, the plastic bag at her side a perfect dancing companion, matching her athleticism with its own elegance. The social worker turns around and climbs the stairs, shaking his head and whooping: "Damn it! You're in trouble! I'm calling SWAT!"

He understands nothing about poetry.

Sugar Child knows even less about halfway house rules. She pirouettes in a counterclockwise circle with her eyes squeezed shut, kicking her grimy feet to an imaginary music's beat.

Four minutes later, a black SWAT van eases to the curb by the halfway house. Three uniformed cops sally from the vehicle, two Mexican women and a pink-faced white cat. The cops saunter toward Sugar Child feigning nonchalance, the way law enforcement officials usually do when they're tense and don't know what they're getting themselves into.

Without any preamble, Sugar Child challenges the first officer. "Get the fuck away from me, man. I haven't done shit to nobody. I'm just doing my thing here." The second cop unholsters her taser. The last cop whips out his baton and wallops Sugar Child in the ribs.

The three officers shove Sugar Child onto the ground— she greets the pavement chin first. The women cops kick her in the head, then roughly handcuff her hands and feet. The white cop jogs to the van and comes back with a long chain. He attaches the chain to Sugar Child's ankles, connecting the remaining length to her manacled hands.

Sugar Child is hogtied.

Trussed like an animal in a stockyard.

She lies in the street, unable to move a muscle. Mascara runs down her cheeks, the wig bereft and friendless on the sidewalk beside her. Next, she's loaded into the SWAT van.

I pull the curtains shut, blotting out what I've just seen. I can't deal with it now. Christ only knows. I limp to the mirror on the other side of the room. I stare into the cracked glass. A bald ex-con with lines of disappointment around his mouth and sorrow in his eyes stares back at me. A middle-aged man in a priest's black robe adorned with cigarette burns. An ill-fitting polyester cleric's collar imprisons his neck. A .25 pistol nestles in his purple sacramental cummerbund.

I draw the .25. I point it at the mirror and smile. The mirror smiles at me, satisfied with the image I present. I restuff the gun in my cummerbund. I pat my pockets, checking to see if I've got my travel permit card and enough change for the bus.

It's time to start my shift.

I'm an ordained priest and professional donations solicitor. I work downtown, where I bang a tambourine and beg for money in the mellifluous, singsong voice beloved by children worldwide: help the needy, give to the poor, amen.

TWO

My bus hiccups through the northbound SWAT checkpoint at Base Line, the traffic behind us nothing but dusty pickup trucks with gun racks. E Street's bail bond offices, liquor stores, thrift shops, and palm trees are aglow in the vaselined daylight, pigeons slanting over the power lines. A wind blows from the desert, inciting clumps of dead palm fronds and empty crack vials to mutiny on the sidewalk.

Exiting the bus on Fourteenth Street, I set up camp by the old McDonald's—the first one in the world. A cornerstone of our civic heritage. I place a white plastic donations bucket on the pavement. I pop a breath mint in my mouth. I spank the tambourine and dance like an organ grinder's monkey to entertain passing Christmas shoppers.

"Help me, help me, help me if you can."

After a slow start, the money is trickling in. A dollar here, a dollar there. Two white guys pause to watch my act. They're tall and pulpy shouldered with long stringy hair. Styling flannel shirts, baggy non-designer jeans, and white sweatshop trainers. Total fashion assassins. You could mistake them for winos—it doesn't take a college degree to see they're plainclothes SWAT cops.

I panic: the .25 under my robe is a surefire felony bust. With my record, good for a dime in the joint. Before I can do anything, the plainclothes men start toward me.

"Hey, hey, Pastor. How's the hustle this afternoon?"

"Hello, boys. You here to make a donation? Your generosity will sweeten a poor child's holiday. A solitary dollar can do it."

The stouter of the two cops, clearly the senior officer, smirks at me. He aims a nicotine-stained finger at the donations bucket. "It doesn't look like you're doing so great today."

"The day is young. My resolve is strong. I have hope."

My inane homilies wipe the smile from his bearded face. "Cut the bullshit. You got permission to be here?"

"Yes, I have god's permission. I'm a priest with Blessed World. The church and charity."

"Yeah, yeah, whatever. You have a license?"

"What are you talking about?"

"Shut the fuck up. I ask the questions. You supply the answers. Got that, dickhead? For your information, you need a license to work this street. You have one?"

I'm ticked off, but given the circumstances, it's best to practice the anger management techniques I learned from shrink sessions in the pen. My answer is restrained, priestly.

"Not on me."

"How do I know you're a vicar or whatever, and not a fucking con artist?"

"You don't."

"That's right, shitbag. I don't. What's to stop me from hauling your ass in on fraud charges?"

"Nothing."

"Right again. You're learning fast. So let's move on. I'll let this slide. But I want something from you." He lowers his voice a tad, just enough to let me know he's thoroughly enjoying himself. "Listen closely, Pastor. Some fuckwad with a gun is robbing banks downtown. He's been seen on E Street. A young dude. Maybe a Mexican. You're out here every day, right?"

"That's my job. It's my volition. I'm trying to—"

"Save the sermon for church. He's gonna contact you."

"Why me?"

"You're a priest. You attract trouble."

"Then what?"

"You let me know, dumb fuck."

"But who are you?"

His hebephrenic black eyes slice into my face. Unblinking, I gaze back at him. Kapow: we're having a full-blown staring match. My strategy—I won't let him punk me. We stay like that for several seconds until he says, "I'm Dalton." He jerks a thumb at his partner. "That's Cassidy."

Dalton kneels in slow motion and fishes three bucks from the donations bucket. My entire take for the day. Pocketing the greasy bills, he stands up with a self-satisfied smile. He and Cassidy then stroll southward to Base Line, a handful of adoring, timid pigeons scattering in their wake.

I watch them disappear into the smog. Disgusted, I spit on the sidewalk. There is nothing in the donations bucket.

I end my shift at midnight. I haven't made one red cent since this afternoon. I'm exhausted, almost delirious, my right hand cramped from shaking the tambourine for the last eight hours. To boot, it's after curfew—I'll probably get rousted at the southbound Base Line checkpoint.

A long time ago my uniform—my robes—meant something important. They were second only to Superman's costume in the hearts and minds of the young and old. They represented a power for good. But the modern world has laid to waste the myths and symbols of yesteryear—I'm an object of ridicule and scorn. A lesser man would be daunted. Not me. Not yet.

THREE

At one in the morning, after negotiating the Base Line checkpoint, I round the corner onto my block. The sidewalk is empty, apart from a lone sneaker orphaned in the gutter. I walk to the halfway house and stop short. The house is dark, the consumers asleep.

Sugar Child's arrest lingers in the air with a magnetic residue that clings to my skin and won't let go. I struggle to remember her face, a heartwarming memory to comfort me at this late hour. I fail, due to the fact she's in the psychiatric lockdown ward at General Hospital on Gilbert Street.

I duck into the California Hotel through a revolving door that deposits me in a near-dark lobby. I wait until the front desk clerk turns his back—I haven't paid rent in weeks—then I sneak across the lobby, making a beeline for the elevator.

The elevator drops me off on the third floor. I tiptoe to my door, unlock it, and step inside a roasting hot two-room suite. My first stop is the kitchenette. There, I peek in the countertop mini-fridge—I'm welcomed by its sole occupant, an unopened pint of plain nonfat yogurt. I take the yogurt into the other room and plunk myself in a battered wingback chair.

I remove the .25 from my waistband. I set it and the tambourine on a three-legged coffee table, the fourth leg a stack of paperbacks. Then I cram the donations bucket under the chair. I dislike the bucket. It's a junkie with a bitter habit. The bucket doesn't like me, either—I didn't bring home any cash. It snarls: you lame fuck. I'm not satisfied with today's take. I need more money. You worthless asshole.

So here I am. Flat broke. For the life of me, I don't know what to do. And I can't get Dalton's words out of my head: you're a priest. You attract trouble.

Maybe he's right.

I flash on the second-to-last time I made love.

I've been out of the pen one night. Back in the world for twenty-four hours. I can't cope with it. There's too many colors, too many people. It's enough to drive me nuts. To relax, I cuddle with my wife, Rhonda, in bed. After a spate of kissing and snuggling, I position myself between her legs. I take her in my mouth. I haven't done this in years. Frankly, I'm rusty.

I tongue her labia. I gently nip her clit. At first, nothing. Rhonda doesn't call my name or go overboard with ecstatic groans. I continue to labor until my jaw aches. I can't breathe; pubic hair and vaginal fluid clog my nostrils.

Finally, she responds with a precious trembling in her legs. I strive onward. I get into a rhythm: tongue up, tongue down. Pause and repeat. It's a wicked formula—she bucks her pubic bone hard against my nose. At long last, she comes. I smile, victorious. I pull myself up into her arms to share the moment. I want to savor it. It's been a long time. Too damn long. But she recoils from me, repelled by my nearness. Curling into a fetal ball, she whimpers: "Leave me alone, please leave me alone."

Shortly after this erotic mishap, my parole officer orders me to find gainful employment. To keep me from returning to the joint. Through the grapevine, I hear about Blessed World.

Blessed World is an evangelical church and nonprofit charity established in the late 1980s. They work with underprivileged communities in the Southland. Their membership is modest—a few thousand parishioners. I apply for an internship with them.

Blessed World's job application form asks if I'm a felon. I don't answer the question. Too risky. Luckily, I'm hired for the secretarial pool. I staple papers, xerox reports, whatever needs to get done. When a slot opens up to be a donations solicitor on E Street, I jump at the chance. I pay a fifteen-dollar fee and undergo a five-day training session. I'm assigned a secondhand cleric's uniform—I rent it by the week. I receive a beribboned certificate that proclaims I'm an ordained priest.

Presto: it's a whole new me.

E Street had been the Southland's second-biggest cruising strip in its heyday. Frank Zappa cruised it. Along with Hells Angels on Harley panhead choppers.

That was a long time ago. The strip isn't famous anymore. But I don't care. I just fantasize how much money I'll bring in. Oodles of cheese. Baskets of it. Thousands of dollars, thanks to my winning personality. Nobody will be able to resist my sales pitch.

Of course, I bring the .25 with me.

□ □ □

I'm ten when my father buys me the .25. He purchases it from a pawnshop on D Street. "You're old enough to own a weapon," he pontificates. "Old enough to learn to use it." With a child's wisdom, I'm ambivalent about the pistol. I'd rather have a skateboard. Yet I religiously practice firing it. Plinking daily at bottles and cans. One summer evening I'm shooting in the backyard. An older neighborhood kid jumps the fence. His zit-embattled face lights up when he spies the .25. "Let me see that thing," he clamors. Cowed by his biological seniority, I hand it to him. Since I've already decimated every can and bottle in sight, there is nothing left to destroy. Providentially, a snow-white rabbit hippity hops into view. A renegade pet that has escaped its owners. "Watch this," he brags. "I'll nick that rabbit in the ear." Lo and behold—he misses by a mile, drilling the bunny's guts. Drenched in its own blood, the animal drags itself under an oleander bush to die. The kid tosses the .25 at me like it's got cancer. "I'd better split," he dithers.

I never see him or the rabbit again. That's my life.

I drowse in the chair while the night spins a path toward morning. The room is hot, but I'm too tired to crank up the air conditioner and too tired to undress. The yogurt has been abandoned on the chair's armrest. I'll have it for breakfast, if it isn't spoiled.

FOUR

SWAT sells authorized internal travel permits—a hundred bucks a pop. You can't buy one if you've got an outstanding warrant, or you're undocumented, or don't have a legal residential address. That means homeless people can't purchase them. Decently forged permits are half the price but don't always see you through the checkpoints. Having no travel card is murder—if you're on the bus and get caught without one, it's a year in county jail. I think that's what happened to Sugar Child.

An excessive heat warning has been issued for today. Children and seniors are advised to remain indoors. I'm eager to catch the afternoon Christmas traffic. So I set up shop in Pioneer Park, eight blocks south of McDonald's. The park grounds are rife with flies, the air smells like ten days in jail.

I play the tambourine with consummate skill.

But I'm not raking in any dough.

Begging for donations is psychological warfare. Some folks can't give alms. I hear their rejections all day long.

Sorry, Pastor. I don't have no cash. I lost my job. My dog is sick. My children have the flu. My wife has boils. I have leukemia. Leave me alone. Get out of my face. Asshole. Faggot. Leech. Fuckhead.

You name it—I get an earful. But I'm a child of Jesus. Vaccinated by his gospel. Ordained by Blessed World. I am spiritually immune to rancor.

A wheelchair-bound man rolls over to me. His hand is out, a bloody bandage wrapped around his blackened fingers. A crusty blue bandanna slants over his left eye. Jailhouse tattoos bifurcate his forehead. The rest of him is bundled inside an oversized North Face goose-down parka held together with duct tape. I suspect he's a recent graduate of Patton State Hospital, the nuthouse by the orange groves in Highland.

"What's up, Pastor? You have a cigarette for me?"

"No, my son. I don't."

"Why not? Everybody smokes out here."

"I don't smoke. It's not salubrious. For body or soul."

"I wasn't asking for a speech. I was asking for a cigarette."

"Well, my child. I don't have any. I'm sorry."

"Okay, okay. You don't have to be an asshole about it. So, you got a quarter I can have?"

"No, I don't."

"Come again?"

"I said I don't have one."

"You don't have a crummy quarter?"

"That's correct."

"You're nothing but a goddamn liar."

"Then we should pray together. To heal our spiritual rift."

"Don't get sarcastic with me, mister. You're here all day hustling cash. You got money. What makes you think you're better than the rest of us? That fucked up uniform? You being a religious figure and shit? You think it makes you superior to me?"

How do I tell him I've eaten nothing since yesterday, other than a pint of nonfat yogurt? That I'm an injured soul just like him? I vent: "Use your fucking eyes. There's nothing in the bucket. When there's nothing in the bucket, there's nothing in my pockets. And when there's nothing in my pockets, I'm in the same damn boat as you."

He does a three-sixty in his chair, and says by way of a farewell before wheeling off: "You don't have to get weird, dude. Shit, I was just talking. Take a break."

I am aggravated. Which is not kosher. I'm usually a barometer of human kindness. But now the barometer is very low. I should pack it in for the day. There is nothing in the bucket. Nothing in my belly.

Then I see Sugar Child.

She's heavily medicated, drifting over the sidewalk with little to no forward motion. Each step the journey of a thousand miles. The walk of patients just released from General Hospital's acute psych ward.

The look on her tired face is interplanetary, as though

she dropped off a spaceship onto E Street. It's clear she doesn't know where she is. She's a visitor from outer space who wants to take off for the stars again. The sooner, the better.

Her eyes struggle to read my face, but she's forgotten the language that once came so naturally. The ability to flirt, to find a place in herself by connecting with strangers.

She tries to remember me—her mouth is pursed from the effort—in the same way a fish comes up from the bottom of a deep pool. Only to reach the top to find out it can't breathe there. That it might be better to go back down the way she came, back to the bottom.

I ache to take her in my arms—but people on psycho-tropic meds hate to be touched. I chirr: "You okay, girl?" I laugh nervously. Tuning in to my discomfiture, she laughs back: "I'm fucked. You know?"

Slow as glue, Sugar Child moves on. I can't stop her. She doesn't want to be stopped. To stop her from walking away, I have to stop the world.

I stammer: "Merry Christmas, baby."

She gives me the saddest smile, a smile that lets me know it's taking everything in her heart to make the gesture. She's doing it for me, with a grace that seemingly comes from the earth itself.

"Merry Christmas, daddy."

FIVE

Seeing Sugar Child in that condition kills me. Her wig is gone. I get back to the hotel, too disoriented to do anything. Later that night a fire starts in the foothills above Devil Canyon—deer and coyote flee down the canyon floor to the North End. At bedtime, I say a Christmas prayer: "Jesus in the manger, in the tiny hamlet of Bethlehem, we're getting our asses reamed out here. Have mercy on us."

I drop into a shallow doze at three o'clock, diving headlong into my very own pond of nightmares—daily life's reconstructed episodes, restitched to fit inside my psyche, like wild animals are stuffed into cages at the zoo. Shazam: my mother is posing in a blue oxford shirt, a plastic bag over her head. Propping a hand on her flabby hip, she sings to me: "You're a big little man. A big little man. You want to be Superman, don't you?"

I dream that my mom makes a speech against the Vietnam War in her high school civics class. It's a stifling hot October

1968 afternoon. The next day she's summoned to a meeting by her vocational counselor, a pasty-faced white man with connections to Campus Crusade for Christ. He wastes no time being polite. "You're against the war. And your family's on welfare, right? You keep up your antiwar sentiments, I'll make sure you never get off welfare or go to college. Now get out of here."

The only doctor in town who accepts welfare patients has an office on Base Line near Tippecanoe. It's in a shabby blue stucco bungalow, minus a waiting room—his patients wait in the dirt-packed front yard, oftentimes all day with smarter folks bringing picnic baskets and umbrellas. Disturbed by the clash with her counselor, my mother visits the doctor. He diagnoses her as hysterical and prescribes phenobarbital, what they give condemned men on death row in prison. Three weeks later, she's committed to Patton State.

□ □ □

I wake up crying, my heart beating faster than a metronome, having slept less than five minutes—if only I could sleep a little more—but it's the greatest moment of clarity I've ever known. I have never felt safe in my life. Not from the second I was born. Not until the day I die. Maybe I'll be safe in the afterlife. I have the strangest feeling I won't.

SIX

I receive a phone call from Blessed World at seven in the morning. I have a new assignment. Good for one afternoon. I marvel at what I'm hearing.

I drawl: "You're joking."

The voice on the horn belongs to a man I've never met, a bishop high up in the church's hierarchy. He tells me it's not a joke. I'm to report to a children's Christmas party on Valencia Avenue in the North End. The organization is short on manpower. No other donations solicitors are available.

I don't like it. The North End is as far away from the California Hotel as one can get in this city and still be in the same town. Getting there will be a hassle. It will take an hour or more. I'll have to ride the bus through the Marshall Boulevard checkpoint. Oh, well. Here I go.

At two o'clock I'm on the westbound bus. I've taken a shower and shaved. My robe is unlaundered. But the .25 is not on me. No need for a firearm at a children's party.

The address I've been given is near the golf course. I'm nervous. Will I fit in? What will the kids think of me? More horrifying, what will their parents think? All I can do is pray everything turns out okay. What I need is the right attitude—I don't think I have it.

I disembark from the bus a hundred yards before the Marshall Boulevard checkpoint. I don't want to deal with SWAT or any of their bullshit, so I cut through an alley. I walk quickly because I can't be late to the party. Sad to say, I don't notice the SWAT security cruiser until it's too late. A trio of cops catapults from the semi-armored vehicle. All in black uniforms, two in sunglasses, the third with an F-19 rifle.

I titter: "Hey, guys, what's up?"

No sooner does the question leave my mouth than the cops grab me by the arms. I'm booted facedown onto the curb; my cleric's collar flies into the gutter. Thank god I didn't bring the .25.

I'm handcuffed, lifted off the pavement, then flung against the security car's hood. Once again, my face collides with an unyielding surface. This time, blood gushes from my nose. But I don't say a word. Nary a peep from me. I know the golden rule: don't speak until spoken to. There I am, beached on the hood. One cop screeches: "Who are you?"

I give him the address of the party and the owner's name, plus a phone number. He radios in the information; the others insult me, saying I'm nothing but a faggot. My contact info proves correct. The SWAT cops uncuff me. They let me go.

My destination is a glass-and-steel mansion. It's new, brand new, more imposing than its neighbors—new money wants to outdo old money. Tech money versus real estate money. The driveway is enormous, the front garden an acre of roses. I press the doorbell by the security gate—I get a quote from Gershwin's "Rhapsody in Blue."

After awhile, I scope out a youngish woman—regal in a purple Dior gown—careening in high heels across the never-ending lawn. She must be coming from the house. The place is so far off, I can scarcely see it.

She unlocks the gate and ushers me into a shaded courtyard. She's all smiles, pretends not to notice the fresh blood on my cummerbund. "Thanks for coming, Pastor."

She isn't polite. That's not her aura. Politeness is the most violent form of sarcasm possible. She's just gracious. And her graciousness puts me at ease. Together, we're old friends. Buddies from the country club, or wherever she hangs out when she's not skiing in Europe.

We stroll toward the house, which gets bigger and bigger the closer we get. It's not a piece of stationary architecture, but an ever-changing optical illusion.

Inside the house my host hands me off to the housekeeper. I'm instantly mobbed by an army of children. They climb all over me, cheering and yelling, pulling at my robe and cummerbund.

I shout: "Merry Christmas, you rug rats!"

The kids burst into war whoops of laughter. They march me into a living room larger than a cathedral. Five stories high with a vaulted ceiling studded by skylights. One corner is hogged by a gigantic Christmas tree festooned with gold baubles and silver lights. Beneath the tree is a hummock of presents wrapped in matte red gift paper.

The children escort me to a low cushioned seat. I sit down. They line up in front of the chair. Then the first kid climbs onto my lap, a tiny girl in a blue silk dress. Her soft brown eyes eat me alive with their innocence.

I ask: "What do you want for Christmas?"

She gets real subdued, stares down at her patent leather shoes, then gazes up at me. "I want everybody to be happy."

I almost burst into tears.

One after another, the kids scrabble onto my lap. They peer into my face, searching for signs of falsity or impurity. When they don't find any, they tell me their wishes. By the time everyone is finished, I'm a complete wreck.

My host reappears in the living room—god knows where she's been. She murmurs: "You were splendid. The check is in the mail. Thank you."

She takes my arm, and with a sly smile leads me out of the house and down a flagstone side path to the front gate. She stands on her tiptoes and pecks me on the cheek. "The children loved you. Blessed World must be proud of your talents. Goodbye, Pastor."

I'm elated—my work is valued. And I did today's job on short notice. There just might be a future for me in this business. I am feeling pretty good—how rare.

Near my bus stop I come across a free box. Curbside free boxes on Valencia Avenue often yield unforeseen treasures. To my delight, I discover a vintage paperback edition of Isaac Babel's *Red Cavalry*. The cover has a full-color reproduction of a 1920s Red Army poster. The book is in mint condition. It's a nifty find. I'm quite pleased with myself.

I wish I could say the crosstown bus ride was as positive as finding the Babel paperback. It's not, and I'm not surprised. At the Highland checkpoint, an outpost bristling with sandbags and razor wire, SWAT personnel halt the bus. All passengers are asked to produce their travel permit cards. That's just how it is. You make do with what you've got. You can't overreach. If you try, you get badly fucked. On the bright side, I pass through the checkpoint.

SEVEN

The telephone rings when I enter my rooms. I'm flummoxed—the phone almost never rings. My only calls are from Blessed World. Is it them? Offering another gig? I don't know what to think. I'm completely shattered, my uniform stinks with blood and dirt. Breathing hard, I grab the receiver.

"Hello?"

"Is that you, man?"

I give the caller a taste of his own medicine. "Who else would it be? The chief of police?"

"Don't fuck with me, asshole."

"Who the hell is this?"

"You don't know? It's Alonzo."

Alonzo is from Waterman Gardens, the toughest projects in town. Midway through his high school senior year, after his teachers urged him to pursue a career as a janitor, he went to the principal's office with a stolen hand grenade and a list of demands from the other Mexican students. The hand grenade didn't work. The administration refused to honor the demands. Alonzo got slapped with thirty-six months in California Youth Authority at Chino. After doing the time, he celebrated his release by getting drunk in Perris Hill Park.

He's been drinking a pint of whiskey every day for years. Only the best brands, he is fond of saying. I haven't spoken to him in six weeks. Not since he went into an evangelical-funded rehab facility in the Del Rosa district.

"Alonzo? What's wrong with your voice? It's scratchy. That's why I didn't know it was you. Do you have a cold?"

"I just had a tracheotomy."

"A tracheotomy? Christ almighty. What's wrong?"

"What ain't? It's my second one in a month. I've got cancer in my throat. Had a damn tumor in there bigger than a golf ball. Now I'm third stage."

Navigating the medical conditions of friends is more dangerous than a battle zone. With every passing decade, our bodies deteriorate and reconfigure themselves into an ever-growing continent of illnesses. Third stage is a synonym for war.

"Alonzo?"

"What?"

"How much do you weigh?"

"I was up to three hundred."

"And now?"

"I'm skin and bones, thanks to chemo."

"What's that mean?"

"I'm down to two hundred."

"That's pretty good. More like you used to be."

"Yeah, well, whatever."

"Are you still drinking?"

"Uh, no. I mean, sometimes. When I was done with that damn chemo, I wanted to celebrate. Then my mom came to stay with me. She was taking out the garbage one day and found a bottle. I lied to her, told her it wasn't mine."

"Why did you do that?"

"I didn't want her to feel bad."

"Jesus, man, what the fuck is going on?"

He adroitly switches the topic. "So what's up with you?"

"You're not going to answer my question?"

"No, I'm not."

"That's chicken shit."

"I won't deny it."

"Okay. Be that way. But things have changed with me."

"How poetic."

"Yeah, it is. I've become a priest."

"A priest? You go to seminary school since we last talked?"

"Blessed World hired me. I paid fifteen bucks for a certificate."

"And that made you a priest?"

"Actually, I'm a donations solicitor. I hustle money."

"Huh? Where's the profit in that? I can't see it."

"I work on E Street. But today I did a kid's party. It was great."

"Sounds fucked up, if you ask me. You getting paid?"

"Yeah. I started as an intern. Now I get a flat wage."

"Hallelujah. What a genesis. Any benefits?"

"No."

"See what I mean? You're getting ripped off."

He's trying to pull me down. It's an old dynamic between us—when he dances in the mire, he expects me to do the same. I don't, I'm an outright enemy. I hate adulthood.

"Alonzo, I'm a felon. I'm lucky I've got the gig."

"Sure, sure."

"And I make people feel good."

"How?"

"I bring mythology into their lives."

"What a load of crap. Totally bogus."

"I believe in myths."

"That makes you an idiot."

"No, it doesn't."

"Then get this. Your dad fought in Vietnam, didn't he?"

"You know he did."

"What did your old man say about it?"

"He said when it ended, the war at home began. The final war. The last war."

"He was realistic. Not like you."

"Don't be shitty, Alonzo. I know you got issues."

"Where did you get that idea?"

"From you."

"How so?"

"You said you're sick."

"So what if I am? And guess what? Rudy from Muscoy wants to speak with you. That ain't good."

Alonzo hangs up on me—I'm paralyzed with the dial tone in my ear.

◻ ◻ ◻

Mormons settled the town during the 1850s. Campus Crusade came here in the early 1960s. My father said when the 1965 Watts riots started, North End white boys slept with their rifles. Alonzo's own favorite pastime is manufacturing reloads for his Colt .38. Nothing brings him greater pleasure than to crimp cartridges at his worktable. Double-notched armor-piercing hollow-point bullets overpacked with gunpowder. Now and then, he looks out the window—his neighbors fly a Confederate battle flag in their backyard. Later he'll inform me: "As history passes through us, we're passing through hell."

And Dalton? He's a cowboy, a throwback to the days when the white boys ran the police department. When only white people lived north of Highland. Black folks had the flatlands west of the freeway. Mexicans south of Base Line.

I'd better watch out for Dalton.

EIGHT

The following morning dense smog from Los Angeles crowns the nearby mountains. A sullen wind gusts through Cajon Pass into the North End, herding tumbleweeds down Fortieth Street. Birds fleeing the still-burning Devil Canyon fire fly over E Street. As icing on the cake, the heat is crucifying me in Pioneer Park. I hold the tambourine above my head and wail: "Purify the day. Give your money away."

To no avail—the donations bucket contains ten cents, two Percocet tabs, an insulin ampule, and one "Vote Trump" campaign button.

My troubles don't stop there. I have to pee so badly, I'm knock-kneed. I wish I were nearer to the downtown public library—I could use their restroom. All the homeless do.

I keep a lookout for Dalton and Cassidy. I don't see the assholes. No sign of Sugar Child, either. However, the Christmas lights in the windows of El Pueblo restaurant are getting strange. Every other bulb, the green ones, not the red ones, are burning out. Six in the last hour. It's how I'm marking the passage of time. When they're all dead, I'll quit for the day.

Like I'm not jittery enough, a nut job by the crosswalk— another graduate from Patton State—is watching me. I ignore him. But I keep picking up on his vibes.

Even in this heat he has a yellow anorak zipped to his neck. A makeshift cape of damaged Christmas tree ornaments covers his shoulders. At his feet is a suitcase, a discolored red cordovan valise. The final touch is the tell-tale bulge under his left armpit. Isn't that cute—I'm not the only person packing a rod on E Street.

He sneaks glances at me, at the ratio of one glance every two minutes, a visual Morse code. The rest of the time, he's scanning the street, nervously eyeing the gold tinsel garlands hanging from the palm trees.

Just when I'm about to lose it—I've got to take a piss—SWAT sirens ping-pong between Pioneer Park and the mall. The high-pitched squeals followed by two squad cars racing toward Sixth Street. As the police blow through the intersection, the nut job reaches under his anorak. He draws a .45 semi-automatic pistol.

The last green Christmas light fizzles out in El Pueblo. That's my cue. Screw it. To hell with it. Enough of this foolishness. Everybody can fuck off. I'm calling it a day. I bend over to snatch the donations bucket. When I straighten up, the cops are gone. The nut job and his suitcase have vanished, too. And I'm glad, because I sincerely do not need anyone's shit in my life right now.

NINE

I drag myself back to the hotel. My rooms are insanely hot, with the faintest taint of a gas leak. The wind rattles a loose windowpane; the sink faucet's drip greets me from the kitchenette. Footsore, I enthrone myself in the wingback chair. I remove the sacramental cummerbund and place it in my lap. The pistol and tambourine are positioned on the coffee table, the querulous donations bucket is at my feet. It's a bad night.

□ □ □

I've been out of prison two weeks. One afternoon—after Rhonda returns from visiting her parents in Barstow—I take a shower with her. The hot-water tap isn't working too good, but the temperature in the bathroom is steamy. And her body heat can set fire to a house.

She recently chopped off her hair, which disappoints me. I like it long. But it's a good cut, done at a ritzy North End salon. Nicely slicked back from her white palisade forehead.

Water streams down her lightly muscled neck to her delicate shoulder blades. Rivulets drain into her cleavage, her breasts perky, the nipples pointed at me, a bar of Dr. Bronner's lavender soap in her right hand. I hope the water gets hotter because we pay the bill.

"Did you miss me?" she asks.

"Of course I missed you, baby. Did you miss me?"

"Yeah. A whole lot."

"How much?"

"Let me show you how much."

She falls to her knees without using her hands. It's an acrobatic feat—the shower stall's porcelain floor is harder than a rock. She bends forward, neck arched, a blue vein pulsing below her jawline. Nostrils flaring, she sniffs me. In one fell swoop, she inserts me in her mouth, taking me to the bristle.

I slump against the stall's back wall, lukewarm nozzle water pounding my skull. I'm not the most well-hung man in the world. Thankfully, she won't gag on me.

But I want to watch myself. I need to see what she's doing. The sight will increase my pleasure—the beauty of her mouth, her eyes tight with beatific resolve. I look for a split second. I gurgle: "Babykins, what's wrong with your back?"

She disgorges me. "What do you mean?"

Her normally smooth back is a field of irritated red bumps. I reach out and touch one. It feels hot and pebbly. "This."

"Oh, that? It's a flea bite."

I repeat after her: "A flea bite? All over your back?"

"Yeah, whatever. My parents have a new cat. When I was there, I slept with it one night. And I got flea bites, a billion of them. They itch like shit. It's fucked up, isn't it?"

"Yeah, it is. Girl?"

"What?"

"I can't do this now."

"Why not? I'm doing all the work here. Just relax. You're always so fucking uptight."

"I know, I know. I'm going crazy. I can't help it."

The moment has gotten too complicated. The parts that made it whole are coming apart. Like an airplane losing a wing in mid-flight.

I shut the water off and weep.

□ □ □

Rhonda is gone. Weeks gone. Long gone. And yet my thoughts stray to Sugar Child. They regularly do when I'm alone and swimming in self-pity. I can still taste her kiss, the piquant tang and texture of her chapped lips. The cough-syrup flavor of her tongue. But now I must sleep; I really must. It's been so long since I slept.

TEN

Last night I mistook a streetlight for the moon. I'm still feeling a little funky this afternoon—the smoke from the Devil Canyon fire is getting to me. But I blame the sun, the damn sun—it never extends a comforting shadow.

The little girl with her dope-fiend mother approaches me in Pioneer Park. I'm surrounded by the donations bucket and a cast-off Christmas wreath I found in a garbage dumpster. The wreath, with its velvety red ribbons, albeit creased with mud, lends a festive zing to my presentation.

The girl clutches a G.I. Joe combat doll, one of the older models. The doll is half naked, missing its pants, a look of distaste engraved on its plastic face. With her other hand, the girl tugs at her mother's army surplus jacket.

"Honey, let go of my coat. You're gonna tear it."

The kid checks me out with an expression that's half Jean Seberg in *Saint Joan* and half Marlon Brando. A facial dialectic hewn from stoic resignation about what the future has in store for her. In tandem with a fount of volcanic rage. All tied together by uncertainty.

Her pinched face belongs to someone who's found out way too young that an awareness of life comes from a proximity to death. In this instance, that happens to be her mother. The woman's long brown hair is matted and unwashed. Her thin patrician features are pitted and scored with moles and wrinkles.

The girl puts on her best tough-guy act. She torques her face into a passable television-gangster scowl. Chin up, eyes blazing. "Pastor?"

"Yes, my daughter? What is it that you need?"

"Can you ask god to bring us a nice Christmas?"

I must not lie. It is a sin. Horribly so. For her sake, I will. "You bet I can. I have the know-how."

"You can get the job done?"

"I've got the tools and the skills."

"How do I know you're the real thing?"

"Because I've paid my dues."

"You're no perpetrator?"

"No additives or preservatives. No MSG."

"For sure?"

I level a first-class stare at the girl, fortified with all the historical consciousness I have at my disposal. A stare that transmits the essentials of my worldview. Read my eyes, child. In our time, identities are permeable, if not inter-changeable. Yet certain truths remain inviolate. History favors the poor. Tomorrow belongs to you.

I whinny: "I'm the real deal. The last show in town."

She lets out a charming giggle. We get down to business. I flip the donations bucket upside down. I lower my haunches onto the makeshift seat. I extend my right arm to her. "Let me help you make your dreams real."

The girl's wee nose burns red with embarrassment. Her mother gives her an affectionate nudge. "C'mon, honey. I ain't got all afternoon. Talk to him, will you?"

She launches herself in one short hop and bounds onto my lap. The kid is surprisingly light. Holding her is like cradling someone who's not completely in this world, but in some other world, too. A place where no one can go unless she invites them.

She looks up at me, peruses the rust-brown bloodstains on my robe. She gives me the benefit of the doubt by not saying anything about them. Then she invites me into that other world of hers with a whiff of licorice-flavored breath brushing my cheek: "I'm Sally. And my mom is Crazy Diane."

The girl's mother, with intuitive streetwise wisdom, has discreetly stepped beyond earshot. She's energetically panhandling a passing tech employee for a cigarette.

"Why is your mother called that?"

"She smokes rocks."

"A lot?"

"When she's got money. And even when she doesn't."

"And where do the two of you live?"

"Pioneer Motel on Fifth Street."

"Where's your dad?"

"Pelican Bay."

I do a tally. Her father is upstate in the pen. Her mother smokes crack. They reside in an SRO motel room. No wonder the G.I. Joe doll she owns looks so rough-and-tumble. Living at the Pioneer is rugged. Cockroaches on the ceiling. No place to cook.

"So what do you want for Christmas?"

I know what she'll say—she will ask for a miracle. She'll demand a world where the refrigerator is always full. Where spaghetti simmers on the stove, an apple pie in the oven. In a pip-squeak trill, she announces: "I want my mom in rehab."

Crazy Diane overhears her daughter's wish. She cackles, visibly pleased, two pink spots on her dead-white cheeks. "That would be a nice gift, sweetie." She then crosses the sidewalk to accost an off-duty bus driver still in uniform. He's got a pint-sized Christmas tree stashed under his left arm. She taps his hand, asking him for spare change.

I want this moment to last forever—Sally holding her G.I. Joe doll. Her mother snickering when the bus driver says, "No, no change here." The wind molesting the empty nickel bags on the pavement. The mad sunlight dappling El Pueblo's windows. Ordinarily, I don't enjoy sustained moments—steeped as they often are in mistakes, problems, and failures. But this moment is a jewel.

I tell Sally: "I can't promise anything. Most rehab places are overbooked. But I'll get on the job, don't you worry."

Satisfied with that response, Sally bounces off my lap and runs to her mother. She takes Crazy Diane by the hand. The saintly child and despoiled mother soldier up E Street to the mall.

I stretch my legs. I sneeze several times. All in all, I'm tickled by my performance. Not bad for a half-assed ex-con. If I could make the day end on this note, I would. Let things rest. Let injured souls make a hegira to happiness. Let the donations bucket brim with gold. Let the tambourine jangle with merriment. Is anyone listening?

ELEVEN

Apparently, no one is listening.

The second Sally and her mother disappear from sight, Dalton and Cassidy materialize by my side. They arrive out of nowhere, how plainclothes men always do, imitating the dead with their quietness. Their flannel shirttails hang loose over sagging gun belts, the wind teases their long hair.

I soothe myself: it's been a glorious day. These assholes are a mirage. They're nothing but a bad dream. I'll kill them tonight in my sleep. You wait and see. I'll kill them good.

Dalton begins our conversation with a sprinkling of insincere pleasantries. "Pastor, it's great to see you again. Really great. I'm stoked."

I lay it on thick in the same phony spirit. "And you, my son. What a delightful occasion this is. Our renewed communion. Worthy of celebration and revelry. All is well?"

"That's what I want to talk to you about."

"Yes?"

"I'm unhappy. Things ain't going too swift."

"I hate to ask. What's the problem?"

51

"Let me explain it to you."

Wordlessly, with a practiced flourish, Dalton reaches out, spins me around, and employs his arm like a nutcracker on my neck. Here we go. Tighten your seat belt. I'm off to the rodeo.

Getting chokeholded, you crave two things. Maybe three. First, you want your feet on the ground. If they're not, you're screwed. Two, you don't want your neck broken. Forget passing out, that's too romantic—you just don't want to die.

Too bad you can't have it both ways. Since I weigh a hundred pounds less than Dalton, my feet say goodbye to the sidewalk without the slightest hesitation.

I dangle inches off the pavement. Dalton is cooing in my ear, "You little shit," like he's reciting a nursery rhyme. But I'm not a little shit. Not me.

Please tell me this isn't happening. That I'm imagining it. That all the hours staring into the bottom of the empty donations bucket is worth it. That when I chant, help the needy, help the poor, pleading with the world until my throat is raw, it's for a good cause. Wasn't I cool to that little girl Sally?

I guess I wasn't cool enough.

I separate my body from my mind.

I'm high above everything. Ahead of me is cottony white light. Isn't that where you go when you bite the dust? I don't want that. Not death. Not now. I switch directions. Soon enough, I find what I'm looking for. A place with no pain.

There are three parts to the picture. Dalton scowling. Cassidy standing off to one side, uninterested. And me, chokeholded in Dalton's meaty arms.

Dalton hisses: "You're an ex-con, aren't you?"

It's not fair, him bringing up the past. And at this particular moment. My personal history is none of his concern—I'm jolted when he mentions Rhonda by her maiden name. The very sound of it turns my stomach.

"Your wife was Rhonda Dukowsky, right? She's a piece of work. You two must be quite a pair. You took a fall for her. What did it get you? A felony conviction. You stupid fucking dork."

One night slightly more than five years ago, Rhonda and I are drinking at La Loca, a neighborhood bar that's been infiltrated by the new tech crowd. She and I are at a corner table with glasses of the house wine. A younger white cat barges into us, causing Rhonda to spill her drink.

Never one to shy away from conflict, she gets in his face, telling him to buy her another glass of wine. He's three sheets to the wind and says no. I advise him to apologize. He bursts out laughing: "You faggot."

Faggot. I've been called that more than my own name. Like the word is printed on my forehead. With people just repeating what they see. To prove they're literate.

When he says it again, Rhonda directs her wine glass to remap his face.

Without any further ado, she and I scatter. It turns out her victim is a prominent tech executive. While waiting at the bar for medical attention, he tells SWAT inspectors he doesn't remember who glassed him, Rhonda or me.

That night the police pull us in for questioning. Right off the bat, I take the rap for Rhonda. I do it out of marital generosity. I do it on impulse, the way I do everything. At first, the cops think I'm lying. A week later I'm arrested. After a lightning-fast trial, I am sentenced to a nickel in the state pen at Muscupiabe for assault with a deadly weapon.

Dalton pokes a finger up my nose. "Where is he, Pastor?"

I sputter: "Who's that?"

"The damn Mexican that's robbing banks."

"I don't know shit."

"Kiss my ass. You're lying. You've seen him."

E Street is the epicenter of the universe—I see thousands of people each day. And I don't judge bank robbers. I accept everyone for who they are. Because everybody is an injured soul.

Dalton drops me onto the sidewalk. I am far away, in a place with no pain. A place where I'm second only to Superman. Fading sunlight stretches in a line across my face. Shadows do not enter the picture. Where are you, Sugar Child?

TWELVE

These aren't the days I'm living for.

Dalton terminates our chat by kicking me in the ribs. Then he and Cassidy turn around and stalk off. Dazed, I manage to roll over and sit upright. El Pueblo's red Christmas lights silhouette me as I telegraph a message to my feet: we need to get the hell out of here.

The growing twilight is perfumed with smog, the opalescent moon a sliver tacked in the soot-gray sky. Women and men attired in formal evening wear are passing through the Mill Street checkpoint on their way to a holiday pageant at the Orange Show grounds. I slink by the shuttered Crest Theatre, recalling the night I saw *Brewster McCloud*. Bud Cort starred as a kid who built a pair of wings so he could fly.

I'm not a star. That's painfully self-evident. Life isn't pretty without lipstick. Yet I've paroled out of prison. And I have a paying job. I also entertain dreams—no matter how flimsy those dreams are, they guide me through shoals of fear and self-hatred. But getting my ass whipped by Dalton is a homicidal truth: I'm boatless in limbo.

A letter from Blessed World awaits me at home. I rarely get mail. I'm surprised by the letter. And I don't like surprises. I take the letter over to the wingback chair. I plop into the seat, the cushions squeaking under my bruised cheeks. Using my thumb, I tear open the envelope. Out slides a single typed page:

THIS NOTICE IS TO INFORM YOU THAT YOUR SERVICES AS A DONATIONS SOLICITOR ARE NO LONGER REQUIRED BY OUR ORGANIZA-TION. THE PERSONNEL DEPARTMENT HAS REVIEWED YOUR FILE. THEY HAVE DETER-MINED YOU ARE MORALLY UNFIT FOR THE POSITION YOU OCCUPY. WE HAVE DISCOV-ERED YOU ARE A FELON WITH A PRISON RECORD. YOUR NAME HAS BEEN REMOVED FROM THE PRIESTHOOD'S ROLLS. YOU HAVE BEEN DEFROCKED. PLEASE COME BY THE MAIN OFFICE TO RETURN YOUR UNIFORM. YOU ARE RESPONSIBLE FOR ITS CONDI-TION. ANY DAMAGES WILL BE DEDUCTED FROM YOUR WAGES. GOD BLESS YOU.

I read the notice two times. I drop my head, blinking back tears. I've been drummed out of the priesthood. And defrocked. Those assholes. Those rotten bastards. How could they do this to me? After all I've been through? Fuck that noise. A sole question repeats itself over and over in my mind: are you going to let them get away with this shit?

For real: I have anger management issues. I have impulse control problems. I suffer from conduct disorder. But the answer is no, I'm not going to let them get away with it.

I have been called epithets. Leech. Faggot. Fuckhead. I've been spat on, punched, and kicked. I have been chokeholded.

It's my uniform, not theirs.

I've earned those colors.

Like the Hells Angels earn theirs.

I keep circling back to that conclusion because I don't know what else to think. Naturally, I'll take my post on E Street tomorrow—my station is as important to me as the uniform is.

But what if the administrators at Blessed World engage in legal action against me? What if they have me arrested for not returning the uniform? Legally speaking, I don't have a leg to stand on. I touch my neck—it's hot and swollen. Dalton can screw himself.

□ □ □

The Devil Canyon fire is climbing the mountainside tonight. Jags of heat lightning boomerang off the valley floor, bleaching the sky from Rialto to Mount San Gorgonio. The answering machine unexpectedly lights up after midnight. I listen to the incoming message:

"Pick up the phone, cabrón. It's me, Alonzo. I want to talk to you. And tell you the things I didn't say the other day. I used to respect you. But you've changed. And I don't dig it. Begging money for Blessed World? That shit doesn't wash with me. You've become a sellout. And you know what? I saw you today on E Street. You sad little pendejo. Banging on that pinche tambourine. Rudy from Muscoy was with me. He said you're a goddamn chump. Don't you know nothing? Look at the people in the street. Just a bunch of hoodlums and ghosts. Who among them is gonna give you a penny? Nobody, that's who. That's basic economics. And besides—"

Exercising its own quirky logic, the machine cuts him off.

THIRTEEN

At sunrise the street cleaners go by my open window. After they pass I crash out on the floor. I awake fifteen minutes later, my neck stiff from Dalton's chokehold. Thanks to the Devil Canyon fire, airborne debris—gray particulate matter—coats everything in the room, including myself.

I stagger to my feet and mope into the kitchenette. I shoo a passel of cockroaches from the stovetop. In turn, they make an orderly retreat into the mini-oven. I fill the coffee pot with water, only to discover I have no coffee, so I drink the water in the pot. Then I brush my teeth with a wedge of bar soap—I don't remember last when I used toothpaste. I can't afford it.

There's no sense in acting like everything is all right today. Because it isn't. With this as my mantra, I load up my pockets with quarters for the bus. I grab my travel permit card—never leave home without it. I gather the donations bucket and tambourine. I'm off to work.

On a smog-free day you can see San Jacinto Peak near

Palm Springs. Similar to an alcoholic, the smog has good days and bad days. This isn't a good day—a flat red haze blankets the desert. The foothills behind Patton State are bald and brown. The sun is shadowless.

I bump into four SWAT cops on the sidewalk. Hoarse screams echo from inside the halfway house— five more cops wrestle a middle-aged blonde female in a polo shirt and Calvin Klein jeans out the front door. Tightly handcuffed behind her back, she jerks from side to side, her white face unfocused in the hostile sunlight.

The cops prod the manacled woman toward a Department of Public Security ambulance idling by the curb. Two medics open the ambulance's doors. The cops push her onto a gurney, the medics strap her down. As the restraints clench around her waist, she screams again, louder than before.

She bares her teeth, save for one missing incisor.

And looks straight at me.

I look back at her.

The SWAT cops twirl their batons like they're drum majorettes practicing for the big Friday night dance. I turn away, older than I've ever been. I flick my tongue over my teeth. Bar soap is caked on my gums—the flesh fails, and the spirit falters. I slouch up the street to the bus stop, one tired footstep at a time.

The Base Line checkpoint is temporarily closed. I'm

rerouted to three emergency checkpoints for vetting. At the first checkpoint the line is long, everybody is quiet. Some folks possess no documents. They can't get to work or home. You get stopped in the streets without papers: bingo. You win the lottery. Three years in county jail. At the second checkpoint a man is handcuffed. I'm patted down by a SWAT inspector in black overalls.

At the third checkpoint SWAT guards ask me for my travel permit again. They look at the card, then at me. My permit is taken to a table where a SWAT tech processes it. The card is returned to me. I notice it has new coding. I ask a cop what it means. He quips, "Top secret." And that's it. I'm free to go.

□ □ □

When my uncle returned from the Vietnam War—after two tours of combat duty—he resided in a garage at his father's house on Sierra Way. For income, he did what everybody in the neighborhood did. He sold pounds of ammoniated Mexican pot. One hundred and ten bucks per pound. The worst weed in the world. My uncle never smiled. None of us did then. Most of us don't now. You don't ever smile at a SWAT checkpoint. Not if you want to get through it in one piece.

PART TWO

THE RETURN OF THE REPRESSED

FOURTEEN

They call me Sugar Child.

I was three years old when my mother took me to a campaign rally in Pioneer Park to see Senator Robert F. Kennedy. It was late May 1968. He showed up in a hurry, just himself and some harried aides. The crowd was a mix of black folks, Mexicans, poor whites like us. The wind was still, the air warm.

Senator Kennedy talked about how everyone was going to get a piece of the pie. Not in heaven. But here on earth. One day our hunger would abate. He reached for people's hands to shake. My mom squirmed to his side. She held me up to him. I was inches away from his tanned face, the auburn hair barricading his forehead. I looked into his resolute and weary blue eyes, his sinewy forearms in rolled-up shirtsleeves. I was colicky, miserable. A fussy little child with food allergies. Days later Senator Kennedy was assassinated in Los Angeles. It was another year before I could eat solid food without throwing up.

SWAT carted me from the halfway house to General Hospital. I was handcuffed to a gurney while a doctor put fourteen stitches in my chin with no anesthetic. Then away I went, down a hallway, through a long white tunnel into hell. In the lockdown unit a shrink asked: "Sugar Child? Are you hearing voices? Are you hallucinating?"

"No," I told her. "But I've got this other problem."

"What's that?"

"I'm in a bad relationship. It's fucking me up."

"Who is this person?"

"A cop."

"Really? Does he reside here in town?"

"No."

"Colton?"

"No."

"Redlands?"

"Nah."

"Then where?"

"He lives inside me."

"Inside you? A policeman?"

"Yeah."

"Does he have a name?"

"Sure does. It's Don."

"Don the policeman?"

"You got it."

"I see. What does he look like?"

"He's a white guy with a razor-thin mustache."

"Do you talk to Don?"

"Night and day. He never shuts up."

"What does he say?"

"Don? He thinks I'm an assbite. But why should I tell you?"

"Sugar Child . . . this is delusional."

"Not at all. Don is real. Too real. The shit he says is just sick."

"How long has this been going on?"

"My relationship with him?"

"Yes."

"We just had our tenth anniversary."

That's when they hit me with Prolixin. A triple dose.

Now I'm doing the Prolixin shuffle in Pioneer Park. Doing the tango of the damned. I've got legs that don't work. Arms that won't move. A mind that can't think. Prolixin reduces everything to static. The only thing I remember about the halfway house—other than meeting daddy—is losing my wig to the SWAT cops.

I'm not proud of that.

The lockdown unit shrink said: "When you feel unsafe, point a finger at the sky. Point a finger at the ground. Point a finger at yourself. Now you're centered. You feel safe."

I don't feel anything, courtesy of Prolixin.

I'm not worried—I have a secret weapon nobody knows about. Not the shrinks, the cops, not Don the policeman, not even the Prolixin knows I command an invisible force field that automatically repels assholes— they just bounce off me.

And look at daddy. Better yet, don't. He's over there on E Street, playing his tambourine for Christmas shoppers.

But they don't care about him—there's no money in his bucket. Daddy is having a bad time today. That makes two of us.

FIFTEEN

I just caught a glimpse of Sugar Child in Pioneer Park—she's the highlight of my day. It's mid-afternoon. I've been hustling for three hours. And I have one paltry dollar in the donations bucket. The bucket is dismayed. It taunts me: you creep. I despise you. Fucking loser.

E Street is a chessboard. I make two moves to my right, I might run into Cassidy and Dalton. I move forward, I'll have a collision with a tech employee. I step in any other direction, I will trample a pigeon.

When you're nervous, everything goes wrong.

I've been nervous since I paroled out of Muscupiabe. Rhonda said it damaged our relationship. But she said that before I got shipped off to the penitentiary. Nowadays? I reckon with nervousness's stepchildren—I wash my hands fifty times a day.

I do it so often, my fingers bleed.

I'll tell you a secret. A terrible one. The letter from Blessed World hurt me. Fuck those unctuous assholes.

They can go to hell. On another level, I have to be honest.
I can't keep the uniform. It's a rental. I even have a receipt
to prove it. They can reclaim it from me whenever they
want. Over my dead body.

In the middle of everything I get wind of a guy with a suitcase at the stoplight. Christ help me. It's him again. The nut
job with the .45. Will you look at his fucking eyes? They're
just like the eyes of the woman that got handcuffed at the
halfway house. Eyes bright from journeying great distances
in his mind, to places that don't exist on any map known to
humankind. I don't need this shit. But that won't save me
from him. He totters to the donations bucket, glances at
it. Now he's fastening those nut job eyes on me. "Pastor?"
    I swing into action. "What is it, little angel?"
    "I'm frightened."
    "Of what?"
    "Everything."
    "Do your travails weigh upon your immortal soul?"
    "Yes."
    "Should we get on our knees and pray for your salvation?"
    "No."
    "Then what do you want from me?"
    He grins, showcasing two rows of irregular sepia-tinted
teeth. Just my luck. I have said what he wants to hear. He
points at his grubby suitcase, the thing bound together
with fraying rope.
    "This is for you."

What is he talking about? And who wants his fucked-up suitcase? It's probably stuffed with body parts from a murder. Or maybe a hundred years of yellowed newspapers.

"I don't want it."

"Please. You've got to take it."

Before I can run for the hills, he pulls a scrap of crumpled paper from his soiled pants. "Read this, Pastor. It's important."

No way. It has to be a message from another solar system where he is the only inhabitant. Why won't he leave me alone? Why can't I just play the tambourine and beg for money?

He sticks the paper in my hand. Then he sets the suitcase in front of me. Without uttering another word, he zips up the street toward the mall.

I pipe: "Wait a second, motherfucker!"

He doesn't look back.

Left to my own devices, I read the note:

PASTOR. I'M IN BIG TROUBLE. I HAVE DONE EVIL THINGS. SOME MAKE ME PROUD. SOME DON'T. BECAUSE OF THIS, GOD IS NOT WITH ME. BUT YOU ARE A CHRISTIAN. YOU ARE CLERGY. YOU MAKE EVERYBODY HAPPY FOR CHRISTMAS. PLEASE TAKE THIS SUITCASE AND GIVE IT TO JESUS CHRIST.

I snort in anger. What total shit. The damn fruitcake. He needs to be in Patton State. I ball up the paper and throw it in the gutter. I glance at the cruddy suitcase. What am I going to do with it? I can toss the thing in the trash, or take it home with me.

A half hour later I pack up my things and catch the bus. The suitcase is bulky, but I manage to get it on board. Fortunately, it's not rush hour. I'm able to nab a seat.

Another donations solicitor sits across the aisle from me. He's tricked out in a sensational uniform. A robe made from flocked black velvet, a cap trimmed with real fur. Boots of kid leather and a silk cleric's collar. His donations bucket is an antique Tiffany bowl.

His belly swells over a gold-trimmed sacramental sash. His cheeks are plump. Plus, there's a humorous twinkle in his green eyes. The bastard—he obviously works the fashionable department stores near the Valencia Avenue checkpoint. Places where people flaunt money. I'm not surprised when he starts needling me.

"Not having any success today, are you, Pastor?"

I flare up, my anger management techniques out the window. "What the fuck is that supposed to mean?"

"You're broke."

"How's that?"

"Your donations bucket is empty. That's sad. Maybe you don't know what you're doing. You want a tip?"

He's laid the bait and set the trap. I walk straight into it. "Yeah, pal, tell me what you think."

"Your uniform is shit. You need a better one. Who do you work for?"

"Blessed World."

"That explains everything. You work for poverty pimps. You paid well?"

"Minimum wage."

"Any health benefits?"

"No."

"You're completely fucked. This is a tough business. If I were you, I'd change professions. Find something easier."

"Easier?"

"Not everyone has the grit to do this job."

He stands up and waddles to the exit, saying over his shoulder: "I've got a party at City Hall. The mayor personally requested me. I'll see you around, Pastor. Don't take any wooden nickels."

The bus drops him off at the corner of Fourth Street. I stare at the suitcase. What am I doing with it?

SIXTEEN

How I got past the Base Line checkpoint was a minor miracle. SWAT removed one passenger from the bus. They were about to ask everybody else for their residential permit cards, but didn't have the time. Which was copacetic, because I've lost mine.

I'm in the hotel lobby strategizing how to evade the desk clerk when Rudy from Muscoy invades my life. Alonzo's cherished half-brother is shirtless and covered in sweat. Par for the course, he's frowning. Rudy detests me. Enough for Rhonda to say he once made a serious pass at her.

"Pastor, I need a word with you. It's crucial."

If Rudy wants to confess his sins, I'll refer him to another member of the clergy—I have no stomach for his woes. Hesitantly, I put down the suitcase. For insurance, I genuflect.

"What is it, my son? Do you need my holy consultation?"

"You know me, Pastor. I'm cool. But somebody else does."

"Do you want to tell me about this person?"

"Yeah, I do. Let me get to the meat of it. You had the fucking nerve to tell Alonzo he has issues. Short eyes have issues. Rapists have issues. Murderers have issues. My brother does not have issues. He is ill. Do you understand?"

"Alonzo isn't dead yet."

"He talks like it. The asshole. He's still drinking. I tell him to cut it out and he gives me some insanity about the air, how bad it is. Like I'm stupid? I don't let my kids breathe the damn air. Do you know how many rehab places Alonzo's been in? That crap costs money."

"What do you want me to say?"

Rudy's sad eyes belong in the frozen vegetable section at the supermarket. "How do I know? Alonzo's so messed up and paranoid, he talks on the phone at home with a loaded pistol in his hand. But why am I telling you this shit? You ain't nobody. You're a fucking charlatan. I don't trust you. And you know what, Pastor? I didn't make a pass at your wife. She made one at me. So fuck you."

Due to Rudy, my vocabulary has a new word. Trust. I swish it around in my mouth, like a fine wine. Nobody ever talks about trust. Rhonda certainly didn't. The philosopher Habermas has written we're living in an age of exhausted utopian energies. I never understood what he meant until just now.

After Rudy and I part company, I venture upstairs to my rooms. A new message is waiting on the answering machine. It's from my parole officer. Telling me he informed Blessed World of my felon status. He's angry I didn't mention it to them. And he wants me to report to his office on the double. If I'm not there by five o'clock, he'll revoke my parole. I press the delete button.

I heave the suitcase onto the coffee table. I settle down in the wingback chair to meditate on it. What if there's a bomb in the fucking thing? There's only one way to find out. I get up and trundle into the kitchenette and rummage around in a drawer for a pair of scissors. Finding them, I return to the coffee table.

Dropping onto my knees, I hunch over the suitcase. Up close, it resembles an Iraq War veteran. The cordovan cloth is scratched and abraded, pocked with blood and mud. If I'm not imagining things, there's a bullet hole in it.

Employing the scissors, I saw through the rope holding it together. The scissors are dull and the rope is stubborn. Right when I'm about to quit, the rope snaps in two. I pull apart the suitcase—three dozen bundles of napkin-wrapped cash tumble onto the coffee table. The bills are in assorted denominations. They gleam faintly sexual, almost extraterrestrial in coloration.

I put one and one together. The nut job is the robber Dalton is hunting for. The cheese has been stolen from banks. For the next hour, I count the dough. When I'm done, I become the unwilling guardian of fifty grand.

Anxiety rappels up my nervous system. I want to wash my hands. To calm myself, I commence deep breathing exercises. Five breaths in, eight breaths out. In, out. In, out. I do this for fifteen minutes.

No dice.

I'm having a category-five panic attack.

Two trains of thought sidetrack me. They override my jangled nerves, beating them back into a corner. For a fact, Superman would never succumb to nervous tension. He wouldn't compulsively wash his hands. And the bank robber's note said to give the suitcase to Jesus Christ. I ask myself the question that lives at the heart of the question itself: what would Jesus do with pilfered bank money?

I'm not the bravest man. Nor am I the smartest. I am a wretched sinner, a defrocked priest. Think hard, I tell myself.

The answer hits me in the pit of my stomach: I cannot be second-best to Superman anymore.

It's many hours later. I'm in bed, too hot to sleep. The curtains rustle—a wiry man jumps through the opened window. He's in military jungle fatigues, a ten-day stubble lays siege to his gaunt cheeks. He has no eyes—two black holes bore into me with a fury greater than the midday sun. It's my dad. In character, he bullies me: "What are you doing with that money? Don't tell me you're gonna do something stupid. I'd hate to think I raised a fuck-up."

Then he dissolves into nothingness.

What I never told Alonzo, what I'll never tell him, the war at home, the one that my father said would follow Vietnam—it'll never end. Not until we break on through to another world. Any world, just not this one again.

□ □ □

I was out of prison two-plus weeks. Sixteen days, eight hours, and counting. Things weren't getting better with Rhonda. In her own fashion she attempts to reunite us. One sultry evening in the kitchenette she says, "Let me give you a hand job." She's smiling, and means well. But I'm irritated from lack of sleep. I reply: "Not now, doll." Rebuffed, she lambasts me with heavyweight accusations, claiming we're incompatible. I clam up, cowering behind a wall of narcissism. Rhonda complains: "Is anybody there?" I answer: "No one's around. Come back later."

SEVENTEEN

I don't know what kind of woman daddy thinks I am—but I'm not the Prolixin casualty he saw today in Pioneer Park. And I am not the halfway-house queen of his dreams. I'm no-man's-land. And from what I've observed daddy is no better. I can only imagine what's he's like in bed. Tentative, probably.

It's past midnight. I'm on Sixth Street. A hot breeze whispers across my skin, rats chitter in the palm trees above me. An unmarked white SWAT sedan rolls up to the curb. Two plainclothes men step out of the car. I stop breathing—the first cop is aiming an orange taser resembling a sophisticated dildo at my nose. The other guy wields a family-size pepper spray canister.

It's party time—I'm the hostess.

I activate my force field. For extra mileage, I point a finger at the sky. I point a finger at the ground. I point a finger at myself. I think pigeons are shitting on my head—the cop with the taser is yelling at me.

"What are you doing here, girl?"

"Huh?"

"I said what in the fuck are you doing here?"

"I don't know."

"You don't know?" He turns off his body cam and smiles. "Maybe you need a vacation in county jail. A visit to our spa."

"You can't do that."

"I sure can. You have no rights."

"Yes, I do."

"Listen, honey. Don't be boring. It's against the law. Just answer my questions. What's your name?"

"Sugar Child."

"I love it. I'll name my dog after you. Guess what?"

"What?"

"This is your lucky night. I'm Cassidy. My buddy is Dalton. We're your newest friends."

"Swell."

"You on meds?"

"Uh . . . yeah."

"What kind?"

I can barely get the word out of my mouth. "Prolixin."

"Tasty. You fresh from lockdown?"

"Yeah."

"You in treatment?"

"No."

"You got your permits with you?"

"Yeah. I just purchased them."

My permits are cut-rate forgeries. Complete hatchet

jobs. I paid a guy on Mayfield seventy-five bucks for a set of residential and travel cards, each valid for six months—they'll never hold up under scrutiny.

"You want to show them to me, Sugar Child?"

"No."

"Why not?"

"Because my permits are good."

"They're good?"

"Uh huh."

"Okay. I'll buy that. You're a nice girl. You stay that way."

The more Cassidy talks, the more Dalton toys with my mind, deliberately pointing his pepper spray canister at my crotch.

I rejoin with a gaze that says: you can't hurt me. My force field is impenetrable. Asshole.

Cassidy interrupts the cold war I have going with Dalton by inviting me on a fishing expedition: "You know that hustler in Pioneer Park? The old man in the priest's robes?"

"Who?"

"The slob that begs for money."

"Don't know him."

"Sure you do."

"Nope. Never seen him."

"I thought everyone knew the dude."

"I don't."

"You shouldn't fib."

"I'm not."

He thrusts, I parry. I'm content with that. Cassidy isn't.

He applies more pressure. Where are you staying tonight? I stonewall his ass. Dalton is pissed. After all, it's a party. And he's having no fun. Then, a voice wafts over us—it's their car radio. All units to Base Line and Waterman. An armed robbery is in progress. A Mexican with a gun.

Dalton winks and says: "See you later, Sugar Child."

EIGHTEEN

I reexamine the stolen cash in the morning—I left it on the coffee table. That was a bad idea. The money looks repulsive in daylight. Deflated by the sight, I go and forage in the mini-fridge. I find a wilted carrot. I gnaw on it. I wash it down with a glass of tepid brown tap water.

The answering machine's blinking red light catches my eye. I walk over to it and punch the play button. Alonzo's drunken rasp knifes my ears: "I know you're there. Trembling in the dark like a culo. Let me explain something. Do you remember my mom? She'd stand in line for hours outside the welfare office on Gilbert. To get government commodity foodstuffs. Sacks of weevil-infested white flour. The temperature out there topping a hundred and five degrees. That's who we are. People with no mythology."

I'm unnerved by Alonzo's message. The tracheotomies have murdered his voice. He's sick, and possibly dying. Yet the prospect of death doesn't mellow him. And he's holding me hostage—in a fraternal Stockholm syndrome. Which only reinforces the bondage-like rapport between us.

I struggle to stay away from the kitchenette sink. But the faucet's bewitching drip is a siren's song. Like a zombie I sleepwalk to the sink. I flip on the hot-water tap. I scrub my hands with dish soap. When I rinse them, my fingertips are pinking with blood. In a trance, I repeat the process. After the fifth time, my palms bleed. Seeing my own blood again—three times this week already—triggers a vicious flashback. To the night the cops took me into custody for the assault on the tech executive.

Rhonda is out getting a pedicure on D Street. I'm alone in our rooms. The doorbell ding-dongs. I yammer: "Who is it?" The answer shortens my lifespan. SWAT police. I do my algebra. I can let the assholes in. Or jump out the window. Rightfully, I select the latter. Only a loser would stick around to get nailed.

It's heigh-ho, up and over the window sill into the wild blue yonder and the pavement below. I don't get far— molecules of anxiety siphon the strength from my legs. Long enough for the cops to break down the door.

The first cop inside shoots me in the hip with a rubber bullet. Pow: I am knocked off the sill to the floor—the bullet leaves a contusion bigger than a jumbo pizza. I writhe on the carpet, happy it can't get worse than this. To prove me wrong, another SWAT cop pepper-sprays me square in the face. A SWAT special operations unit brings in a robot—a toy-sized metal box on four wheels—to sweep the rooms for contraband. Then I'm taken downstairs to the lobby.

Initially, I am transported to a substation north of Base Line. A bunch of SWAT tac squad cops in the booking room take one look at me and chorus: "Kill the faggot, kill the faggot."

Brilliant, I muse to myself. Truly brilliant.

I'm thrown into the holding cell with a drunk Mount Vernon hustler. A bit of rough trade. Irate because he's been socked in the jaw by the desk sergeant. He grips the bars and screams he's in pain and wants to see a doctor. Three officers charge into the cell to whale on him. Within seconds, there's a stew of blood and skin on the walls.

In the middle of the night I am cuffed and driven in a patrol car to county jail. I'm escorted into another holding cell. Still handcuffed, my clothes are taken from me. I'm moved again—dumped nude in a strip cell. Nobody knows where I am. Maybe no one ever will. My balls shrivel with fear as plainclothes detectives interrogate me. One claims he's a lawyer to get me to confess. I say zilch. What's there to admit? That Rhonda went for a pedicure? Nope. That's not me.

At dawn I'm issued a regulation orange jumpsuit and transferred to a felony tank. I'm fortunate enough to score an upper bunk. I also discover a John Dos Passos paperback novel hidden under my smelly plastic mattress. The book has no cover and looks as if someone used it to stop a bullet.

The paperback is a welcome diversion—the tank's toilet is backing up. It's regurgitating fecal matter from our tank and the other tanks in the jail. We're getting everything. Nonstop.

I bury myself in the novel, reading fifty pages until the warders order me from the tank. They yell: "Leave the book behind!" Shoeless, I slosh through watery shit to the gate. I'm shackled and chained to a string of other prisoners. We're corralled to court for arraignment.

I make a grand entrance into the courtroom, tracking brown footprints. I spot Rhonda among the spectators in the pews. My baby girl. Her loyalty is breathtaking. I try to smile at her. But I can't. My mouth won't cooperate. Because my bail is set at one hundred thousand dollars. I can't afford that or a private attorney, so I'm assigned to a public defender. A young pup who doesn't know squat. He's convinced a jury of my peers will convict me. Opting for the alternative, we go to trial by a single judge. Next stop: Muscupiabe.

It seems wrong to think about these things now, but memories are deceitful. They have a habit of showing up like cockroaches when you least expect them. I simply cannot forget how the curtains came down on Rhonda and me.

I've been out of prison three weeks. Rhonda is in our walk-in closet, jamming clothes into a suitcase. From the doorway I bleat: "Why are you leaving me?" My question is an exercise in rhetoric. She's already spelled out her departure's catechism. It's summarized in three words—I'm an asshole.

She lifts her valise, assaying the stockings, towels, panties, and bras she'll ration in the days ahead. Then she looks at me, sniggering: "Do you want me to say it again? You're an asshole."

I did a nickel for this crap? No, I did not. I wag my head, indicating she's not going anywhere. Rhonda gingerly places the suitcase on the floor. Bam: she springs at me, raking my face with her fingernails. I lurch backward. Whoa. What the fuck. She hoists the valise and flits from the room. Her high heels clack with terrifying finality out the door.

In agony, I reel into the bathroom. An unsympathetic mirror confirms what I fear. I'm the reluctant owner of four deep and symmetrical bloody claw marks on each cheek—stretching all the way down to my chin. Rhonda always pampered her nails, encouraging them to grow into steak knives. I'm aghast. Will my face heal, or am I going to look this way forever?

For the next week, it's touch-and-go. The claw marks don't blanch. Rhonda doesn't call. Alonzo comes by, but his visits bring an alcoholic's uncanny knack for jabbing at what hurts most. He has a solemn, canonical liturgy: "I never approved of your old lady. Never did. She's a North End white girl. She isn't the kind to stick around when the shit hits the fan. Yeah, okay, okay. She didn't divorce you while you were in the joint. But that's fucked up. She was waiting to do it when you got out. She's passive-aggressive. You're better off now. You don't have to worry about her stabbing you in the back. But your face is totally ruined. I'd see a dermatologist if I were you."

□ □ □

The phone is ringing again. I steel myself. It's got to be Alonzo. Asshole or not, he needs my support. I shut the faucet, leaving bloody fingerprints. I sashay into the other room. I pick up the receiver and gabble: "Alonzo? You all right, man? Listen, it doesn't matter what you think of me. I don't care if you disrespect me. I'm cool. I mean, it's Christmas. And if things get—"

A canned voice breaks in: "This is a prerecorded message from the law firm of Dougal and White. We represent Blessed World. Your former employer. You are being contacted in regard to your usage of their property. Your refusal to return a uniform estimated in value at three thousand dollars is now a criminal offense. Because of the aforementioned item's worth, this is a felony, punishable by incarceration. Your ongoing usage of the apparel for purposes of soliciting money also constitutes a felony. This message is to advise you to cease and desist. You have twenty-four hours to return the uniform to Blessed World's office. Any other action on your part will be construed as adversarial. If you plan to return the uniform, please press one. If you have questions and wish to negotiate the surrender of the item at a later date, please press two. If you—"

I slam the phone down, my blood pressure skyrocketing through the ceiling. Who do those punks think they are? Nobody talks smack to me and gets away with it.

Consider my résumé. It's an alphabet of jails, handcuffs, palm trees, smog, and pepper spray. I don't have friends in high places. I don't know the mayor like that other donations solicitor does. So what. I'll get by.

NINETEEN

I amble downstairs, still peeved about the message from Dougal and White. The clock in the lobby says it's one hundred degrees. I exit the hotel—I'm late for work.

A small knot of consumers are talking and smoking by the halfway house steps. One has a broom and is sweeping butts from the gutter. He finds a choice one, sticks it in his mouth. Another consumer, a diminutive Samoan woman in a recycled surgical gown, buttonholes me. "Hey, Pastor! How are you this morning?"

I check the tubercular brown sky, the sun hiding behind a skein of tissue-paper clouds that stretches from Little Mountain to Waterman Canyon. My neck is killing me—I couldn't swallow the carrot I had for breakfast. I squeak: "I'm maintaining. You?"

She repays my question with great news. "It's the best day of my life. I just got accepted into a treatment program out in Highland. Near Patton. I'm going there this afternoon."

"Very nice. For how long?"

"Twenty-four months."

"That's a considerable stint. A big deal."

"My insurance pays for the thing."

"How marvelous. Merry Christmas, sugar."

The consumers laugh at me. Most wear plastic intake bracelets from Patton State. The oldest of them sees me looking at his bracelet. Annoyed by my curiosity, he takes his lit cigarette and expertly flicks it at my robe. Sparks dance around my feet. I'm too tired to protest. So I just leave.

□ □ □

I walk south on E Street to Fifth Street, and over to Seccombe Lake. It's hot and muggy—I have no deodorant. At the lake I watch ducks cavort in the oily water.

I hear a crow cawing. I swivel my head. A monstrous black bird is sneering at me from a lakeside tree. My skin turns cold with dread—crows caw at me and SWAT cops and lawyers have memorized my name. I recite a self-prescribed rosary: pain explains life better than love does. Jesus in heaven, please help me get through this day. That's all I fucking want.

TWENTY

That's right. Today is another opportunity for me to mess up. Or get things straight. Which way I'll go, I don't know. It's a toss of the dice. Between the donations bucket and myself stands an abused Christmas tree. I found it abandoned in Pioneer Park. A motherless tree with no decorations on its emaciated branches. Apart from the tarnished gold star fastened to its balding crown.

I've been talking to it for hours. "Do you need water? Some presents underneath you? Or boys and girls to smell your bittersweet fragrance?"

I hurl the tambourine in the air. Without looking, I catch it behind my back. The .25 pops out of my cummerbund and clatters onto the sidewalk. Two pigeons inspect the gun, pecking at the barrel. I threaten them with the tambourine—the filthy, loveless birds fly off to El Pueblo's garbage dumpster.

A tiny crowd has gathered to watch my routine. Two tourists from Germany named Roland and Greta.

They drop a dollar in the bucket. Roland says in heavily accented English: "You are authentic, Pastor."

Greta takes my photo with her cell phone. Inspired, I break off knee drops and full splits. I fall into the Swim. I execute the Funky Chicken. I throw the tambourine in the air again. I do a double-take: Sugar Child is leaning against a parking meter, puffing on a cigarette.

Wherever Sugar Child has been in the last twenty-four hours, it wasn't around here. But in some other dimension where there is no oxygen. She is thin, the weight loss centered in her face. A spotty, wan face drawn with the ineffable knowledge she's leaving this world quicker than it's trying to keep her.

She models a pair of mismatched cardboard slippers, the kind you get in the Salvation Army detox unit. Her dingy sweatpants are held up with a bungee cord, over which hangs a blue work shirt. Robbed of the wig, her hair is nubby.

I catch the tambourine on its downward flight. I raise my arms in an unspoken prayer. I'm not asking for money now. I am not asking for anything one human being can give to another. I'm asking for more than that. I want every power in this universe, every wind, every ray of light that comes to rest upon this desperate land, to have mercy on Sugar Child. To give back what's been taken from her. I am asking for joy in a world beyond redemption. For whatever can be conjured from the ordinary, to renew this tired earth.

When I'm done praying, I look at Sugar Child. As if I've

been hallucinating, she's gone. Greta stops taking my picture. "Pastor? You seem perturbed. Are you all right? Yes?"

Her accent is thick, but less pronounced than Roland's. I respond with pure organic silence: no, honey, I'm not all right. Far from it. I am in a wilderness.

Roland and Greta bid me a rousing goodbye, promising to send a postcard from Germany. It's a perfect time to get lunch, maybe at the soup kitchen in Pioneer Park. Even better, I can visit the public library restroom.

I look at my newly adopted Christmas tree. A tree so brave and fucked up, I cannot help but love it. I brace myself against a trash can. I nod with my eyes half-closed, the sun on my face.

I glance at my hands—they're shaking uncontrollably.

I'm jarred from my reverie by a homeless wino. He's pushing a lopsided baby carriage piled high with a sleeping bag, a slew of decapitated Barbie dolls, and two shoeboxes bulging with plastic jewelry. A shorthaired cat sleeps on top of the pile.

The wino himself is enrobed in a black long-sleeved collarless dress. On his head is a gaudy blue-and-red scarf held together with a yellow safety pin. His hair is long on one side, shaved to the scalp on the other side. He removes a pint of port from the purse hanging around his neck. Uncapping it, he takes a slug, then dries his lips with a sleeve.

"Pastor, I want that Christmas tree. It ain't yours, is it?

I like it. I like it a lot." He soaks me up with his one good eye; the other orb is so wall-eyed, it stares at the sky. "And no disrespect intended, Pastor. But your robe's been massacred. You can't go around looking that way."

"Pretty bad, huh?"

"The worst. A disgrace to your office."

"Yeah, well, I don't have money to fix it."

"That's no excuse."

I've neglected to sew my robe's rents. I'm embarrassed by how disheveled I am. But the more the robe disintegrates, the freer I become. By the time it's completely unwearable, I'll be a free man. It's a perverse thought. I don't want to pursue it. I steer the conversation back to the tree.

"You want the tree?"

"Yeah, I do. Let's negotiate. I'll give you a Vicodin for it."

"I could use a good buzz. Is it fresh?"

"Straight from the factory." Digging in his purse, he extracts a once-white chalky tab that has seen better days. He proffers it to me. "It'll fuck you up."

"You gonna give me a refund if it doesn't get me high?"

"Don't sass me."

I look at the Vicodin. I look at the cat asleep in the baby carriage. I look at the pickup trucks chugging in the street. I mull over the wino's offer.

"Keep the tab, my child. The tree's all yours."

The wino walks away with the Christmas tree. For once, I'm at peace with myself. I have been defrocked—a decisive blow to my self-esteem—yet I remain a servant of the people. The lambs in the street. I must avenge their hunger. I must slake their thirst. I must try, and try again.

TWENTY-ONE

I shouldn't obsess about daddy. It's just that every time I see him, I get sad. Him begging for money in those raggedy robes. I've never met a man who was stronger than a woman. Looking at him, I never will. That's all there is to it.

I cinch the bungee cord yoking my sweatpants, then I do the latest installment of the Prolixin shuffle up E Street, my cardboard slippers swishing on the pavement. I get a hundred yards before a rat jumps from a palm tree. My force field repulses it—the rat misses me and hits the sidewalk. I point a finger at the sky. I point a finger at the ground. I point a finger at myself. I keep shuffling.

The Blessed World Church is on Arrowhead by the old courthouse—it's in a rundown suite at the rear of a desert-style deco office building. I shuffle through the entrance into the reception area. Past tables stacked with dog-eared AARP magazines. Past rows of pastel orange cubicles, each one with a consumer and their social worker. I stop at the last one.

"Rick? I'm here."

My caseworker slams shut his desk drawer—but not fast enough—I see the dime bag in it. I know he's shooting dope because he wears a goose-down parka indoors when the room temperature is triple digits. I'd love to see his arms. Two to one, he's got tracks from here to Canada.

"Sugar Child. It's wonderful to see you."

Rick ushers me into his cubicle like an old maid fussing over her dying cat. There are potted palms and wind chimes, a dwarfed white aluminum Christmas tree standing sentry in the corner. I settle onto a couch with no cushions. I haven't bathed in four days. My hair is nubby. My eyes are screaming. Don the policeman chuckles: you're damn ugly with no wig.

"How you doing today, Sugar Child?"

"Kind of weird."

"You look like shit."

"Great. I feel better already."

"Let me get you booked into a treatment program."

"No."

"Why not? You need to get off the street."

Rick drones on. All I hear is the drip-drip of his voice in my head as a curtain of Prolixin dullness washes over me.

"This isn't good." Rick's tone downshifts from convivial to clinical—the gears in a two-tone personality. "You sick? You got hep C?"

"No."

"You sure? You don't have to lie. Everyone has it. It's nothing to be ashamed of. I've got it, if you want to know the truth. It's no big deal. I'm on antiviral medication. I get acupuncture. I take Chinese herbs. I'm doing fabulous."

"I tested negative."

"Congratulations."

"Thanks. That means a lot coming from you."

"I'm here for you, Sugar Child. I am committed to your reentry into society. But you need to get into treatment. At Blessed World we have a saying. You know what it is?"

"No."

"Treatment is liberation."

"Okay."

I squint at him. I'm not into elaborations—why wear a dress when you can go naked? I have no idea where he shoots up. He can't do it in the bathrooms here because they have security cameras. And he doesn't seem like the type to hit up in the street. Too prissy.

"That's it for now, Sugar Child. I have more appointments and stuff. You can see yourself out."

Instead of leaving the building I make a detour into an unlit hallway. There's not much to look at. Conference rooms. Single-stall male and female restrooms. All the doors are locked except for one. Abracadabra: I slip into a storage closet overflowing with Christmas donations.

Toys, dishes, tuxedos, rice cookers, lawn furniture. One box shelters a floor-length silver lamé ballroom gown with frayed spaghetti straps. A magnificent garment. Fragile, yet brazen. Audrey Hepburn. Stuffing it in my sweatpants, I hobble back into the hallway and ghost past the security guards at the front door to the street.

Outside, dusk cloaks E Street—an enchanted fairyland where goodness grows on palm trees and the sidewalks are paved with food stamps. Don the policeman is outraged: you're a jerk. What the fuck is with you? Why didn't you get any SRO housing vouchers from Rick? I want air conditioning. I want it now.

TWENTY-TWO

I tune out Don the policeman as I wander to D Street and hang a right onto Wabash. There's a party in a bungalow just past a curbside bamboo grove—-unpenned chickens are running loose in the driveway. The first person I run into there is an overweight Mexican cat with a bandage around his throat. He's white as a ghost, his eyes black and mad with terror. He flirts with me: "Don't I know you from somewhere, chica? My name is Alonzo. I'm from Waterman Gardens."

My mom used to sell acid on Base Line. In her apartment—I was living with my grandparents—she had six refrigerators. Each stocked with different kinds of acid. Blue double-dome tabs weighing in at 275 micrograms apiece. White paper blotter at 230 micrograms. Her masterpiece was a gram of gray mini-barrels—four thousand hits—taking the cake at 307 micrograms per hit. The acid was clean, she never cut it with speed or strychnine. Of course, certain customers complained. One of them was this very same Alonzo. I heard he ate five tabs of the blue double-dome and skydived off a rooftop and broke his legs.

Alonzo doesn't recognize me—he's too busy describing his tracheotomies. He offers to exhibit them. I decline the invitation. He changes subjects and talks about the June 1970 Jimi Hendrix concert at the Orange Show. A riot broke out. Cops fired off tear gas. Hendrix quit playing. Then it's when Arthur Lee and Love played at a club on E Street:

"Arthur Lee took the stage in his pajamas and bathrobe. He didn't smile. Neither did we. His eyes electrified us. He had the ultimate knowledge—it was a fucked-up night. And tomorrow would bring even more crazy shit. He was our conscience."

Alonzo falls quiet; starlight bathes his pale face. A Harley panhead rumbles on E Street. Now a SWAT helicopter shaves the treetops, enveloping the bungalow in retina-damaging yellow light. A loudspeaker blares:

THIS IS AN ILLEGAL GATHERING. YOU ARE SUBJECT TO ARREST. IT IS CURFEW. REPEAT. IT IS CURFEW. FAILURE TO DISPERSE WILL RESULT IN JAIL TIME. REPEAT. IT IS CURFEW.

Without saying goodbye to Alonzo, I vamoose. I skirt the chickens in the front yard. My cardboard slippers kiss the sun-warmed sidewalk as I float down the street to Pioneer Park with the day's sadness flowing though me—I let it suckle at my breast. Hush my sorrow. Cry no more.

I rest on a bench in Pioneer Park, watching the moon sink behind the heat-whitened mountains. I sense a pair of eyes and glance up—a rat in a palm tree is frowning at me. Don the policeman whinges: there's too many mosquitos here. Let's go to Seccombe Lake. It's nicer there. I snap: shut up, will you?

I wonder where daddy is tonight. We could've ridden off into the sunset together with me on the back of his saddle, my arms knotted around his waist while I inhaled his spicy smell. Don the policeman jeers: fuck you, girl. That man is a loser. And you're a two-timing whore. I rail at him: I don't need no cop telling me what I am. You old fart.

□ □ □

None of this would be happening if I had my wig. You can quarrel with your man. Even slit your wrists. Maybe go to hell. But don't ever lose your wig. You'll regret it. And no matter how divine the silver lamé gown is, it'll never turn me into Audrey Hepburn. I'm on my own now. And I don't know anybody who isn't.

TWENTY-THREE

The day after I see Sugar Child, my bus is marooned at the Mill Street checkpoint. SWAT cops with F-19 rifles have eight men spread-eagled on the ground. The unprepossessing checkpoint has no razor wire, sandbags, or anti-truck barriers. No techs to process internal travel permits. It's just a ramshackle glass-walled toll booth. But people have been shot here. I'm breaking out in hives—I would give anything to wash my hands. Finally, everyone is vetted. We get the go-ahead. Forward to the promised land.

I find a cluster of clergymen and street people standing by an altar of candles and wilted flowers in Pioneer Park. They're honoring a homeless woman who died the night before. Someone says it was near El Pueblo.

The street people uncork bottles of wine and pour libations onto the pavement. To send the deceased into the afterworld with a taste of fortified port.

A priest intones: "Oh, holy father, in thy august and sacred name, receive this child of yours, as she has left the

Southland to be in your arms. Love her and cherish her, as this city did not. Take her into your flock."

While the priest finalizes his eulogy by saying, "Whether we are rich or poor, god in heaven will always console us," gunshots erupt near the bus stop. Two shots from a large-caliber pistol. On its heels is the report of a smaller handgun. I look to my left. The bank robber that gave me the suitcase is highballing down E Street's center lane. Without stopping, he lifts his .45 and fires a single shot— it wings a stoplight, killing it on yellow.

Right behind him are Dalton and Cassidy.

Dalton aims his service revolver at the robber's back and squeezes off three rounds—the first slug clips a woman in the arm as she exits El Pueblo, the others gouge a palm tree's trunk.

The robber dashes onto the curb, crouching near a fire hydrant. Pivoting, he steadies the .45 in the crook of his elbow and shoots. Cassidy is blown off his feet, a fountain of blood geysering from his neck. Fighting gravity—his knees buckle inch by inch—he capsizes to the pavement.

Dalton skids to a halt and levels his revolver. He fires: the bank robber's head disappears in a nimbus of blood and bone fragments. The shot's blast—riding high on the wind—echoes for a long second. Until Dalton's triumphant falsetto cuts through it: "I killed the little asshole! Yes, I did!"

The winos in the park had been cheering the robber, exhorting him to make his escape. They shut up when

Dalton wheels on them; the narc's beard is speckled with blood.

"Fuck you, faggots! Fuck you! I'll kill all of you!"

Within minutes E Street teems with SWAT vehicles. The block is quickly cordoned off with yellow crime-scene tape. Cassidy's body is bagged and hefted into a coroner's van. The robber is left in the road—one cop after another kicks his still-warm corpse until it's just a heap of skin and rags festering in the December sun. His spirit, a near-transparent whirlwind of dust and frond bits, takes flight, lifting over El Pueblo. I shade my eyes against the smog's glare and watch it disappear from view.

I learned to say the Pledge of Allegiance in kindergarten. I placed my right hand over my heart and repeated the sacred oath: one nation under god, indivisible, with liberty and justice for all. But when I see the bank robber's brains pooling in the gutter, and when I hear the priest cursing at my side, I know god is indifferent to us. I know the devil rules E Street.

Dalton strides back and forth in front of the coroner's van. A uniformed officer throws an arm around the plainclothes man's shoulders. Dalton nods, then wipes his eyes with the back of his hand.

I have to go before the maniac sees me.

TWENTY-FOUR

The dead man is baking in the street—green flies feast on his face. Dalton and the other SWAT cops are searching his pockets. Daddy is standing by his lonely self at the corner. How bald he is. How little hair he has left. Don the policeman chortles: that guy is a stone-cold sap. Piss on him.

God help you, daddy. Don't you understand anything? Your hair has to be correct, along with the rest of you. I say that with kindness. But I won't wait forever for you to get it together.

I want to cry—the Prolixin won't let me.

I double-check to make sure the silver lamé gown is safe in my sweatpants. Then I see an agitated and shirtless man storm past the police line. Next thing I know he's cornering me in El Pueblo's parking lot. It's Rudy from Muscoy.

"Sugar Child! You check those damn shootings? No? Myself? I can't stand this shit no more. But I gotta calm down. I just gotta."

Death scares Rudy. I see that in his slightly crossed eyes, how shiny they are. But death doesn't scare me. I've always been close to it. Rudy talks faster: "Anyhow, where you been lately?"

"I was in lockdown."

"Yeah? I'm sorry to hear that."

"I got through it, more or less."

"Where's your wig? That platinum beauty queen thing."

"SWAT confiscated it."

"Wow. That's vindictive. What dogs. You gonna sue them?"

"Stop it."

"Fine. Fuck it. I'll keep the sympathy I got for all living things, including your wig, to myself. All I gotta do is remain calm. Now look here. Alonzo talk to you?"

"Who?"

"Alonzo. My brother. The fat fuck."

"I don't know the cat."

"He met you last night. At some weird-ass party."

"People talk shit."

"You saying Alonzo's talking shit? You ain't the only one."

"I'm not saying anything."

"Good for you. That's wise."

"Yeah, right."

"So let me ask you something else. See that douche bag across the street? The beggar with the bucket? He ain't no priest. He ain't nothing but Alonzo's friend."

"I told you. I don't know Alonzo."

"Fair enough. You win. Christ, it's hot."

Don the policeman wheedles: I'm hot, too. Can we at least get in the shade? I retaliate: no, we can't. I am not going to stand under a palm tree and wait for a rat to jump on my head. Don lashes out: you sorry piece of shit. Is that your only option? We could be indoors with air conditioning. You negative asshole.

Rudy butts in. "Sugar Child?"

"What?"

"You talking to yourself?"

"No."

"You sure of that?"

"Sure, I'm sure."

"Then who you talking to?"

"Don the policeman."

"Who's that?"

"My boyfriend. We're having a fight."

"You and him squabble a lot?"

"All the time. We've been at it for days now."

"When you ain't fighting, he treat you good?"

"No, never has."

"Why are you with him then?"

"I don't want to be alone."

"That bad, huh? Sometimes you have to separate the wheat from the chaff."

"You should be a psychiatrist."

"Damn straight. And you know what else? I'm going to Los Angeles. Gonna take the Greyhound there."

"How come?"

"To get away from this mess. Maybe go to the beach. Work on my tan. Meet some movie stars. Only problem is, the bus takes a million hours."

"I want to go, too."

"Why don't you?"

"Gangs at the beach, they'll punk your ass."

"I ain't afraid. I'm from Muscoy. And I can't even swim."

"That your secret weapon?"

"It is."

"People are weird in Los Angeles."

"And what are we?"

I look at him through Prolixin eyes. "Different."

I take leave of Rudy and plod up E Street. Pigeons wing to and fro above the palm trees. The overheated air jumps with mosquitos and flies. The sun beats on my head with a violence that makes me doubt I am alive—it's possible without my knowledge or permission I have died. And this is the underworld: pickup trucks with gun racks. Pedestrians stooped from heat fatigue. Smog thicker than ice cream. Don the policeman guffaws: you don't know anything. You're retarded.

I brood about daddy—if only he were handsome. Don the policeman crows: I heard that. You think the bald-headed motherfucker is better than me? Wrong. No one will put up with your shit the way I do. Who was with you in jail? Who was there at the halfway house? And in lockdown? Do I have to spell it out? Without me, you ain't nada. Plain and simple.

The Prolixin has failed to stop Don—it's done little to suppress his appetite for abusive repartee. Somehow, I've got to rid myself of his madness—if just for a day. That's not much to ask for, but it's too much to think about right now.

My caseworker Rick? He doesn't know what to do with me. He says: treatment. I've seen people after treatment. After the twenty-eight-day program. Twenty pounds overweight from eating surplus government commodities. Medicated to the gills on mood elevators and psychotropics. Hands shaking like birds' wings. Forget treatment.

TWENTY-FIVE

I stare blindly through the bus window as SWAT guards in flak vests wave us by the Base Line checkpoint. My seatmate, a Catholic schoolboy, susses me: "You okay, Pastor?"

I cannot stop trembling.

My block is status quo when I get there. Outside the halfway house a social worker counsels a female consumer swaddled in a ratty chenille bathrobe. "Look, princess, you can't be down on yourself. You're doing great. You've made a lot of friends in this place. Your discharge papers are in order. And you're gonna get into the treatment program you want. You're fine. It'll be a great Christmas this year."

Maybe the social worker is right. It will be a good Christmas. But my homecoming is marred by a letter from the offices of Dougal and White. I rip open the manila envelope it comes in. I blaze through the missive:

THIS IS YOUR FINAL WARNING. IF YOU PERSIST IN ILLEGALLY RETAINING PROPERTY THAT DOES NOT BELONG TO YOU, OUR CLIENTS AT BLESSED WORLD WILL HAVE NO OTHER RECOURSE THAN TO TURN THIS MATTER OVER TO THEIR SECURITY DIVISION. THE NORMAL PROCEDURE IS FOR THEIR INVESTI-GATORS TO CONTACT YOU IN PERSON. YOUR PAROLE OFFICER HAS BEEN ADVISED OF THE SITUATION. THANK YOU.

I tear the letter into shreds and toss it out the window. An updraft captures the paper, propelling it into the air. Up and down, round and around.

At dinnertime I wash my hands in the kitchenette sink like there's no tomorrow. Then I trudge into the other room. I turn on the overhead lights. I'm rewarded with a gruesome sight—my hands are crusted with blood. It's a case of obsessive compulsive stigmata.

As a bonus, the upstairs neighbor is beating his dog again, something he does with alarming regularity. The mutt keens with an agonized howl that rips through floors and walls. My mood takes an unexpected dip, shifting from black to blacker. Maybe it's the killings I saw today. Or the letter from Dougal and White. Maybe I don't need a reason.

I reach under the wingback's fusty cushions for the .25.

The pistol gleams like a toy squirt gun in the light. I check the clip—to make sure it's full. I flick off the safety. Next, I stick the muzzle in my mouth and curl my index finger around the trigger.

Nobody knows what happens when we circle the drain. Possibly we leave this existence for paradise. Or maybe we don't. If I squeeze the trigger, I hope my destination is pleasant.

Diagrammatically, the bullet will tear through my palate, the short journey ending in my brain. I won't die—the .25's slugs are too puny. I'll merely collapse to the floor without ceremony or pomp. Blinded. Unable to talk. Incapable of movement. A vegetable. I won't remember Sugar Child getting hogtied. I won't know who Rhonda is. For the rest of my days I'll be sequestered at General Hospital.

August 2000. I'm in General Hospital with shingles. The guy in the next bed is a Hells Angel named Frank. He shattered his leg—his panhead crashed into a tree in Del Rosa. He's a cool dude, generous with his Newport cigarettes. He also has a portable AM radio. Together we listen to Thin Lizzy, Marvin Gaye, and Sammy Hagar. His mother and two younger brothers visit him every day. The brothers are a pair of hulking blond cats in black leather vests and engineer boots. Miniature versions of Frank. Their mom is a blue-collar madonna with bleached ringlets and a pierced nose. She chain-smokes her own brand, mentholated Marlboros. Nice people.

Much of my life is behind me now. Memories delude me into thinking there's more to come. But the only thing I can rely on is the past, and even that's turning into quicksand. I pluck the .25 from my mouth. I put it on the coffee table. In all honesty, I don't want to kill myself. I just think I do.

The donations bucket watches me from its spot under the chair. It curses: you pathetic asshole. I want more money.

I pay no attention to the bucket. Instead I gaze out the window. The North Star shines brighter than a disco ball in the polluted black sky. The moon waxes over Mount San Gorgonio.

□ □ □

The hands that play the tambourine. The eyes that saw Dalton shoot a man dead. The tongue that reveled in Rhonda's private parts. The ears that listened to the better-dressed donations solicitor say I was fucked. The mouth that chants, help the poor. The nose the SWAT security cops bashed into the pavement. The nerves that shake whenever I go through a checkpoint. The stomach that lives on carrots and nonfat yogurt. The hair that fell out in prison. The neck Dalton chokeholded. The skin scabrous from the desert wind. The brain that thinks about death. The lips Sugar Child kissed. The heart that beats frantically. This is a hymn for my body.

I go downstairs and step outside for a breath of fresh air. I start coughing—the northwesterly wind brims with creosote and smoke from the Devil Canyon fire. To deter looters—the mall was vandalized the other night—a camouflaged SWAT armored personnel carrier is parked by El Pueblo. I stand on the sidewalk, motionless, numb, snug inside my cocoon of woe.

As I reenter the hotel two cats shoulder past me into the lobby. One is tall and black, the other short and white. The short cat wheezes at me: "My name's Rick. I'm a caseworker for Blessed World. This guy," he gestures at the other man, "that's Andrew. He just got his meds and needs to start taking them. So who are you, the security guard? If you don't mind, we're in a hurry to get inside and begin his paperwork."

Andrew holds a Walgreens bag of prescription drugs, his passport to a better world than the one he's coming from. I want to explain to him there is no better world. As usual, I'm wrong. I simper: "Rick? You know where you're going?"

"Sure do. This is the halfway house, isn't it?"

I take in the lobby's potted cacti, the desk clerk giving

me the evil eye. I look at the sky varnished by smog. I witness a shooting star over Cajon Pass. I make a wish on that star, that one day everyone will find their way home.

"No, it isn't. The halfway house is next door."

I go upstairs and pad into my rooms. I take a moment to dwell on the life of Italian theoretician and writer Antonio Gramsci. He served a long stretch in the pen. His wife waited for his release. Rhonda was not interested in that kind of lifestyle. Alonzo says she's currently residing in posh Santa Monica—scored herself a rent-controlled condo near the beach. On that note, I shut the lights and hit the sack. Hopefully, my father will visit me tonight.

I wait, wide-eyed in the blistering dark.

But he never shows up.

TWENTY-SIX

The headlining story in the morning's paper says SWAT's Lieutenant Chet Dalton has been placed on administrative leave. An inquest into the shooting deaths of Sergeant Rico Cassidy and the bank robber is pending. The robber has not yet been identified. Another article reports the Devil Canyon fire is marauding south into the North End. Wildwood Park is in flames. The golf course, too. The police have ordered the evacuation of upper Valencia Avenue.

□ □ □

I stow the stolen bank cash in a food-stained Vons grocery bag. I put the bag by the door. Okay. I'm almost ready to hit the street. Maybe I should take the .25 with me. Just in case of an emergency. There are pros and cons. If I bring it, I might shoot someone. If I don't, somebody might shoot me. Debating the issue with myself will take all day. I forget about it when the telephone jingles, portending bad juju.

I lift the receiver in fear. "Yeah?"

A female voice with a glossy Central American accent unleashes a blitzkrieg of consonants and vowels: "Pastor? Alonzo needs to talk to you. He's no good. You be nice to him."

It's Alonzo's wife, a woman from Nicaragua named Josefa. I complain: "I can't talk now." Nonetheless, the phone changes hands. Like a malfunctioning satellite, Alonzo flames into my orbit: "What's up?"

I nearly shot myself in the head last night. I am violating my parole terms. Self-doubt is my middle name. I tell him, "Not a whole lot. I was just going to work."

"Fuck that job. Remember you ain't getting any younger."

"Talking to you is always so uplifting."

"Don't mention it. Hey, you know Sugar Child?"

"I do. I mean, kind of. I'd like to know her better."

"I met her at a party the other night. She's totally rad."

"A party? I'm envious. Where at?"

"This crib on Wabash. SWAT came and shut it down. I don't know what happened to Sugar Child."

"Were you drinking?"

"Yeah, I was. I got shit-faced. What's it to you?"

"Nothing, nothing. I was just asking."

"That Sugar Child is a trip."

"How is she? Did she seem okay?"

"What do you mean?"

"She's been having problems."

"Well, I was drunk. I can't say how she was doing."

"That's great."

"Yeah, give me a medal. Listen, I was thinking about your dad. What's up with him?"

"He drove his car off the mountain a few weeks ago."

"And your mom?"

"She's in Patton again."

"That's fucked."

We submerge into a protracted silence. My father is newly buried in the cemetery at Highland and Waterman. I'm certain his first night there was unsettling—the place will take some getting used to. And dear old Mom wrote me a letter just before her return to Patton. She said I was a disappointment. A failure. And I would always remain one.

"You mind if we talk about something else, Alonzo?"

"Sure thing. Rudy said he ran into you."

"More like shrapnel hit me."

"Don't listen to him. He keeps talking about going to Los Angeles. You want my verdict? Rudy has mental health problems. He's stressing."

"He's stressing on you."

"You think? Anyway, here's the reason I'm calling. I ain't doing well. I want a stem-cell operation to get rid of the cancer. My doctor said I had to find someone who's compatible with me. For a tissue donation or whatever. I asked my sister. She was the best candidate. So she gets a blood test. We find out she has hep C. I'm back to square one."

"What about Rudy?"

"He's got it, too."

"Jesus. What're you gonna do?"

Alonzo's uneven breathing is overdubbed with a response so slurred it might as well be a message in a bottle that's crossed an ocean to reach my ears. "This is my plan. The cancer is getting too aggressive. I have to go back for another round of chemo. But I've already done that. The truth is, if I can just have ninety days without doctors or pain, that's all I need."

"And afterwards?"

"I'll check out. Leave this crap behind."

"That's it?"

"What? You need a menu? I'm tired. Isn't that enough?"

"I don't like the sound of it."

"Whose life is it? Yours or mine?"

"Let me guess. Yours."

"Exactly. So shut your mouth."

"I don't know about this."

"What's there to know? Please don't be a pendejo. Can you do that for me?"

"I can try."

"And there's something else."

"What's that?"

"I want you there."

"Where?"

"At my bedside when I go."

Alonzo is nominating me to be his designated driver—

to row him across the River Styx. Though he'll never cop to it—he wants me to die with him. It's understandable. Alonzo dislikes being alone. He keeps talking: "Campus Crusade used to flood my high school with their propaganda. You couldn't walk down the hallways, there were blizzards of it. It was white-boy hell."

Not every public high school is converted into a private evangelical academy. But Campus Crusade has pull in this town. A few years after Alonzo went to the principal's office with the hand grenade, his school was privatized. I'm not suggesting the grenade had anything to do with it. I am not saying these circumstances pushed Alonzo toward alcoholism. Somebody composed a poem and didn't finish it—they had Alonzo in mind.

"Alonzo?"

"Yeah?"

"You talking to me with a gun in your hand?"

"How did you know that?"

"Rudy says it's your thing."

"The little snitch. Fuck him."

Alonzo and I say goodbye. I have to go to work.

I take the elevator down to the lobby, and I walk outside into the soul-destroying sunshine. Just past the hotel I'm confronted by sewage from the halfway house. It's churning through a hole in the sidewalk. The house's youngest consumer—a skinny cholita in tight brown slacks and a cropped leatherette jacket—inspects the spillage with scientific curiosity. She sagely opines: "This is some creepy shit. I wouldn't eat it. Not in a million years."

We're joined by an older consumer, a heavyset white woman palsying like a leaf in a wind tunnel. She produces a half-smoked Marlboro cigarette butt and torches it. "Guess what, Pastor? It's my birthday. I'm forty-seven today. And I've got MS. You know what I want? I want to go to Disneyland, the one in Orange County. That would make me happy. I haven't been there since I was sixteen."

I add her to my roster of injured souls.

□ □ □

Should something go wrong on the job today—this is my last will and testament. I leave you the .25. An extra clip of bullets. The rent I owe. My sleepless nights. I bequeath the smell of the orange groves. My parole officer's telephone number. I ask you to remember: I wore my robes in Jesus Christ's sacred name.

TWENTY-SEVEN

I get a psychotic headband of dizziness when my bus oozes through the Sixth Street checkpoint—and I die a forgettable hypertensive mini-death. I can't take it no more. I really can't.

An undersized, dun-colored coyote with the weathered face of a homeless wino—a Devil Canyon fire refugee—skips in front of the bus. The beat animal skedaddles across E Street, vanishing behind a palm tree. We're three blocks from the mall.

I alight from the coach on Fifth Street with the Vons bag, tambourine, and donations bucket. The sun is crapping out in the smog; a moody wind rampages over the sidewalk, driving orange peels and crack vials to El Pueblo's doorway.

At Pioneer Park a woman in overalls is serving bowlfuls of vegetarian goulash to a soup kitchen queue of winos, mothers with children, and the undocumented. I sidle over to the first person in line, a lanky white man in a patchwork denim shirt. I reach in the Vons bag and dredge up a sizable chunk of twenties. I offer him the money. When he takes it, I approach the next person, a woman with three kids. She snaps up a mound of bills from my hand. I walk down the line, dishing out more dough. If I believe there'll be a fairy tale ending here, replete with hosannas, I'm mistaken. As I fork over cash to a Mexican lady, she frowns at the fivers I've given her.

"Pastor, why are you doing this?"

No way will I tell her the cheese was given to me by a half-insane bank robber. And I won't say I'm pretty crazy myself—I'll keep that gem under wraps. But she wants to know my unholy grail?

I've been post-trial in county jail for three months— waiting to get slotted into Muscupiabe. One day I hear a ruckus in the adjacent tank. Three guys affiliated with the Brotherhood have a kid on his hands and knees. A slender young sissy who's squealing through the athletic sock stuffed in his mouth. One holds him still; the other two are taking turns carving his face with a sharpened tooth- brush. Another Brotherhood associate slips behind me, his home-cooked-meth stink breath roiling past my nose: "Mind your own business, pinhead. Unless you want to end up like sissy boy in there."

A trustee stands outside my tank in the morning. He holds a hand mirror sideways, letting me see the most recent doings in the next tank. It's a new chapter from the prayer book of hell. With ecclesiastical calm the sissy sways from the butt end of a knotted wifebeater tied to the bars, his feet an inch off the floor. His once-pretty face is marbling with early rigor mortis. No longer earthbound, his mouth is upturned in a smile: I'm free. You assholes aren't.

For a heartbeat, I'm jealous.

Nobody cuts him down. No one wants to get written up for tampering with a crime scene, resulting in the denial of commissary privileges.

I could be up there with him, the two of us dancing together into purgatory. But I wouldn't smile. Not like him. It's just not the style. Not where I come from.

My credo: each to his own. I distribute forty-five grand of pharaoh's money at the soup kitchen, divvying the cash to my lambs on a flyblown, sweltering afternoon—off to the promised land we go. Superman would never approve of me, but that's his damn problem, not mine.

TWENTY-EIGHT

But like I said, there was no fairy tale ending. A black SWAT helicopter banked over Pioneer Park, then circled back for another look. That was enough for me. I tossed the empty Vons bag on the ground. I wired a command to my legs: it's time to go. With the tambourine and donations bucket firmly in hand, I peeled through the park's crackheads to E Street.

I'm weeping from exhaustion when I get there. Mother of Christ. In my worst dreams I couldn't have asked for a messier day. Sick of everything—defrocked—I strip off the tattered cleric's collar, cummerbund, and robe. I jettison the rags into a garbage bin.

Still crying, I chuck the donations bucket onto the pigeon-shit-caked pavement. I'm trying to figure out what to do next when two muscular blond men in blue Brooks Brothers suits and yellow suede Hush Puppy loafers flank me. Unfortunately, I know who they are. It's not stellar news. The taller one asks: "You the donations solicitor?"

I'm coy. "Who are you? You guys evangelists or what? If you're evangelists, I got no time for you. I'm busy."

"We're investigators from Blessed World."

"What's that? A theme park?"

"You don't know? We're a charity. And a church."

"Is that a fact? I've never heard of it."

"We've come for the uniform. It's our property."

"Come on." I laugh hysterically through my tears. "You see me wearing anything like that?"

As the robe came apart, I shed the husk of the person I once was. The man they seek no longer exists. The fool that wore the uniform is gone. I laugh harder, snot leaking from my nose. "I don't know who the fuck you're talking about."

"But what's that bucket you've got?"

"What about it?"

"And you have a tambourine."

"I'm the best damn tambourine player you'll ever meet."

"You don't have our uniform in your possession?"

"What's the matter with you, man? Are you blind?"

"Have it your way. We're calling SWAT."

"Oh, yeah? That's fantastic. I can't wait."

I shut my eyes. I see Sugar Child shimmying in front of the halfway house. I see the Isaac Babel paperback in the Valencia Avenue free box. I see little Sally and Crazy Diane in their room at the Pioneer Motel warming a can of soup on a two-burner hot plate. One thing is certain. I stick around here, it's a ticket back to Muscupiabe.

I deep-breathe. Five breaths in, eight breaths out.
On the ninth breath, I reopen my eyes.
I take off like Superman.

I jet past ancient Mexican women hawking canned goods on the sidewalk. Picking up speed I hightail it past El Pueblo, the footfall of the Blessed World investigators lagging behind me. In mid-stride I pry the last of the bank robber's money—taped inside my tambourine—and pitch the bills into the wind.

Five thousand dollars spiral in the wintry sky, mingling with blackbirds and pigeons sidewinding over the rooftops. Caught in a downdraft, the banknotes plunge to the ground.

I cross Sixth Street against a red light. A cloudburst of sparrows blows up over the power lines as a bus pulls away from the curb. Sprinting alongside the coach, I motion at the driver to stop. He slows down and opens the door. "What the heck is wrong with you? You trying to get yourself killed? Get in here and sit your ass somewhere in the back where I don't have to look at you, okay?"

I clamber aboard and flutter to the rear. A black woman in an orange babushka counsels me from her seat. "Young man, you're buck naked. If I were you, I'd pray for deliverance."

I take her advice. While the bus rattles north on E Street, I kneel in the aisle on a bed of apple cores, used syringes, plastic bags, and toilet paper. I pound the tambourine and sing:

"For every injured soul. To whatever can be conjured from the ordinary, to renew this tired earth."

TWENTY-NINE

I haven't seen daddy for a little while—but I'm distracted—SWAT cops are running around in all directions. When no one's watching, I sneak behind the dumpster at El Pueblo. I wriggle into the silver lamé gown. It's more work than I thought—the damn thing fits me tighter than a straitjacket. But whatever. The price is right. I'm looking good. Wig or no wig.

□ □ □

It'll be a wonderful Christmas—I just know it. Never mind the heat. The rats in the palm trees. Or Dalton. Or Rudy from Muscoy's mania. None of that matters now.

Delighted with my silver lamé gown, happier than I've been in ages—my blood sings—I'm veering into Pioneer Park when something brushes my shoulders. I look up—cheese is raining from the skies. I lift a hand—a ten-dollar bill attaches itself to my fingertips. All at once I see Robert F. Kennedy in the park. He's in gabardine slacks, a white dress shirt, no tie. His mussed auburn hair is movie-star perfect. Brandishing a fistful of twenties, he declares: "There is fear we will never be truly free from hunger and want, from illnesses which eat the soul, that we are nothing but fodder in history's mouth. Yet we are nearing Jerusalem. If not this season, then the next. For the meek shall inherit the city."

His voice fades into a Prolixin hiss. I hike the gown's hem and shuffle to E Street. One step, two steps. The sidewalk glimmers with smashed Christmas lights, gold tinsel drips from palm trees. I'm nearing Seventh Street when a northbound bus passes by with a naked man on board. He's banging away at a tambourine like some kind of escapee from Patton.

I blink twice. Oh, daddy. What are you doing?

THIRTY

Look at it this way: it was a crapshoot. The odds were against me. But it's nothing to worry about. I just have to live my life. Hold my head high. Do the best I can.

You have saccharine thoughts like that when you're hand-cuffed and naked in the backseat of a SWAT squad car en route to county jail. The cops up front are laughing about how easy it was to bust me. That a nude man on E Street isn't hard to pop, even if he's hiding on the bus. The ass-holes—they took my tambourine.

The SWAT car zooms by El Pueblo. I peep through the back window, admiring the garden I planted. Twen-ty-dollar bills impaled on tree branches. Ten-spots lolling by the curb. Homeless folks are pouring out of Pioneer Park to harvest greenbacks from the sidewalk.

I'm not alone in the backseat. I've got plenty of company. An entire orchestra. Rhonda is the loudest: I don't under-stand you. That time you went down on me? It was dreadful.

Bad technique. Bad everything. Instead of talking with me, instead of just being tender, you tried to control me. And I freaked out, didn't I? It's all your fault. It always was. You ruin everything. Alonzo is merciless: I invested much too much into our friendship. All that energy, all that love, completely wasted. Do you know how selfish you are? No, you don't. You're a narcissist. Rudy from Muscoy spews: Rhonda not only made a pass at me, she put her hand on my you-know-what. I'm not lying, dude. Your wife did that. While you were in prison. So go fuck yourself. The bank robber goes for my throat: I told you to give the suitcase to Jesus Christ. But you had to give the cheese to a bunch of homeless pendejos. You betrayed me, puto. Dalton chirps: I've got great news, Pastor. The district attorney is going to throw the book at you. And I can't wait to get you into the strip cell. Just you, me, and a pair of brass knuckles to redesign your pious face. Superman gets in the last word: you tragic fuck. How could you compare yourself to me? Look at you. This shit would never happen to my ass. Not in this lifetime. And there's only one Superman. That's me. Not you, asshole.

Here it comes. Christmas Day at county jail. No visitors. No bail. The felony tanks reeking with Lysol. The toilets brimming over. A tin bowl of congealed oatmeal and margarine for dinner.

And no Dos Passos novel this time around.

Let's be reasonable. I have to get the fuck out of this car.

Like pronto. There's only one way to do it. Five breaths in, eight breaths out. In, out. In, out. Now go: I head-butt the backseat's metal security screen. I lacerate my scalp, bleeding on the floor. Perfecto. The SWAT cops bawl at me to stop it. Boom: I butt the screen again. Pissed off, the driver brakes the squad car, double-parking just past El Pueblo. His partner vaults out of the vehicle, trots to my door. He unlocks it, then reaches for his taser.

You ever been tasered? You'll do anything to avoid it. Anything. Short of begging for mercy. Which only makes the pricks want to taser you even more. The SWAT officer rips open the door, looms like a werewolf in the backseat. I feint to his left. He flinches—all that blood on me. I lunge past him and somersault onto the pavement.

It's showtime.

I pogo to my feet and dart up the sidewalk. A SWAT foot patrol sees me coming—they race to cut me off. They're in single file, orderly, and silent. I'm intimate with their parochial silence: it's rubber-bullet time. The worst of times. A volley is fired in my direction—the air glistens black with rubber.

Hampered by the handcuffs, I leg it toward El Pueblo. At full tilt I stumble and crash into the eatery's windows, ramming my forehead through the double-thick panes—the plate glass breaks into shards. Shaking off blood, I skid into the dining room, dancing barefoot in broken glass. I leapfrog onto the nearest tabletop as more SWAT cops breeze into the restaurant. I kick a salt shaker and ketchup bottle at them. Then I get a load of Sugar Child in the doorway. Standing proudly alone. Just killing it in a silver lamé ballroom gown. A frayed strap hangs from her bony pale shoulder. Her nubby hair is greased with Vaseline. SWAT cops tackle me from behind—I receive a double blast of pepper spray in the eyes. Playing hard to get, I broad jump from the table onto the floor. I shoot by the startled cops and head out the door into the street. I turn right, rushing toward Base Line.

□ □ □

I'm running faster than punk-ass Superman ever did when an unexpected coolness touches my face—the sun passing behind a palm tree—and for a delicious moment everything is new again. The sky is indigo blue. The mountains sparkle. Nothing has been lost. No one is a loser. And it seems all my problems will end, that I'll never revisit loneliness or pain, but the end is very far away, and the last war is just beginning. I run through the street, crazed from pepper spray, shouting: "Sugar Child! I love you! I really do!"

But rubber bullets are flying everywhere, and nobody hears me, nobody at all.

PETER PLATE taught himself to write fiction while squatting in abandoned buildings. He is the author of many books, including the novels *Police and Thieves, Angels of Catastrophe, Elegy Written on a Crowded Street, Soon the Rest Will Fall*, and *Dirty in Cashmere*, all published by Seven Stories Press.

SEVEN STORIES PRESS is an independent book publisher based in New York City. We publish works of the imagination by such writers as Nelson Algren, Russell Banks, Octavia E. Butler, Ani DiFranco, Assia Djebar, Ariel Dorfman, Coco Fusco, Barry Gifford, Martha Long, Luis Negrón, Peter Plate, Hwang Sok-yong, Lee Stringer, and Kurt Vonnegut, to name a few, together with political titles by voices of conscience, including Subhankar Banerjee, the Boston Women's Health Collective, Noam Chomsky, Angela Y. Davis, Human Rights Watch, Derrick Jensen, Ralph Nader, Loretta Napoleoni, Gary Null, Greg Palast, Project Censored, Barbara Seaman, Alice Walker, Gary Webb, and Howard Zinn, among many others. Seven Stories Press believes publishers have a special responsibility to defend free speech and human rights, and to celebrate the gifts of the human imagination, wherever we can. In 2012 we launched Triangle Square books for young readers with strong social justice and narrative components, telling personal stories of courage and commitment. For additional information, visit www.sevenstories.com.